THE EDINBURGH HEIR

Edinburgh Seer Book Two

ALISHA KLAPHEKE

Text copyright © 2018 by Alisha Klapheke
Cover art copyright © 2018 by Damonza

Library of Congress Cataloging-in-Publication Data
Klapheke, Alisha
The Edinburgh Heir/Alisha Klapheke. —First Edition.
Summary: Fate chose Aini MacGregor and Thane Campbell to change the face of Scotland forever and lead an unconventional rebellion using supernatural elements.
ISBN 978-0-9987379-9-7 (trade)
ISBN 978-0-9987379-8-0 (ebook)
[1. Fantasy. 2. Magic—Fiction.] I. Title.

Printed in the United States of America
10 9 8 7 6 5 4 3 2 1
First Edition

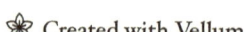 Created with Vellum

~

To my sister, for cheering me on

~

CHAPTER 1
SUGAR-COATED PLOTS

Aini popped the hard candy into her mouth and waited for her feet to leave the ground.

"How does it taste?" Thane was heating another batch on the stove, but his gaze kept straying from Aini to the window.

The lane curved away from the lonely rebel safe house that was serving as their temporary living quarters. The small town of Greenock, just northwest of Glasgow, exuded the sleepy feel of a good long, nap, but Aini knew better than to be lulled into a lack of vigilance by its quaint charm. At any moment, Campbell kingsmen would spring out with guns blazing.

"It tastes fine. Maybe a little less sweet than normal. So you're sure Nathair didn't tell anyone other than that group?"

The temporary lab's overhead light blinked across his glasses as his chest moved in and out. "That's what I overheard when Rodric spoke to him over the phone. Just before Bass Rock. Said he wanted to keep this all quiet until the right time."

Aini's head began to feel a bit funny. She went to the window and the late summer chill seeped through the glass and into her fingers. Despite it being only the very beginning of September, the trip from Edinburgh to Greenock had been flecked with what felt like winter rain. She drew the curtains and took a breath, watching Thane and Myles work.

"What is that face you're making?" Thane pushed his blond hair away from his black-framed glasses and eased the thermometer into the bubbling sugar.

"I was just wishing I didn't like the new lab so much."

At the townhouse in Edinburgh, the lab had been tidy—she'd obsessively wiped the long, metal table and the marble countertops—but the building had been ancient. The whitewashed walls still showed pitted rock and they harbored dirt she could never quite clean.

This lab was tucked into the guest house kitchen of a twenty-year-old home. Smooth walls. Electricity a person could rely on. Stools, windowpanes, and drawers made in this century. It was heaven.

"I feel guilty that I love it so much," she muttered.

The old lab had been home and here she was mixing candy, doing experiments, and whistling merrily as home sat far away in Edinburgh, alone and dark. Well, maybe she wasn't exactly whistling merrily, but the rest of it was true.

Gold stubble shone on Thane's sharp chin and along the curve of his jaw. He rubbed at it with his tattooed fingers as he studied the temperature of the hard candy mix. It was odd to see him with a little scruff. But it made sense that he'd forgotten to shave or hadn't felt like bothering with the routine. Nothing was routine anymore. Aini simply chalked it up to yet another difference in this man standing in front of her. He was no longer a spy. He'd gone against his own kin to save those he believed needed his protection. This was the new Thane. And she was the new

Aini. Both of them in hiding, and on the surface as well as beneath the skin, they were rougher, brighter—more.

"Guilt will get you nowhere, Aini," Myles said, responding belatedly to her confession and looking around the lab she was trying not to enjoy.

She gave him a smile. "You're right, but I can't stop feeling it, or worrying about when they'll find us here."

Her fingers were drawn to the Adam's apple moving in Thane's strong throat. She curled them there for a second, enjoying the warmth of his skin and the beat of his pulse. A small smile pulled at his mouth as her feet left the floor.

Her stomach dropped as she focused on rising, floating—any thought that would lead to breaking gravity's hold. A little light-headed, she rose and rose and rose.

"Um..." The floor was suddenly very far away.

Thane reached up a hand and grabbed her shoe. The black flat slipped off and he held it gently. "You all right?"

"I guess." The ceiling's ivory paint was smooth under her fingers.

Myles clapped once. "Well! That is a record height, isn't it?"

"It is." Aini put a hand to her head. A mix of fear and plea-sure ran through her body. It was great they'd made such a successful altered sweet, but she wasn't so sure she could control this. How would it help them in a fight if she just floated away like a balloon?

"Is it making you sick?" Thane's eyes pinched with worry.

"Not really. I just feel...odd."

"Can you move around?"

Imagining the air was water, she moved her arms and feet and aimed for the arch of the guest house door.

"I don't think that's working so hot," Myles said.

He was right. She needed to pinpoint the way she usually

controlled her movement while under the candy's influence. Her tongue clicked against her teeth as she thought. She normally just looked at the place she wanted to go and her body obeyed, floating lightly over the floor. Maybe she simply had to focus a bit more now that the candy's effect was stronger.

The spot between Aini's eyes almost seemed to hum. Zeroing in on the sensation, embracing the feeling, she mentally "pushed" out from that point, toward the door. She sped over like she was on a zipline from the buzzing spot on her head to the door's archway.

"You figured it out," Thane said. "This will be great for visuals on a larger field of battle."

"Field of battle." Myles rolled his eyes, but it looked forced. Was he afraid? If so, she didn't blame him.

"It will," Thane said. "You'll be able to see who needs help and you'll be able to get away from enemies."

"Not if they have flyers." Myles clamped his lips shut.

Thane glared.

Myles held up his hands. "I'm sorry, but seriously. She'll have to be really careful about that."

Now Aini did feel sick. They were so not ready for this. She focused on the ceiling's peak and drifted like a leaf in the wind, her short dress shifting against her ribbed leggings. With a spin, she reached her arms wide and surveyed the makeshift lab in its entirety.

Thane's mouth had fallen open. Myles elbowed him, and his lips snapped closed.

"You do look really amazing up there," Myles said. "Like some kind of avenging angel."

Aini couldn't help but grin. "I like that."

Myles shoved Thane so he was directly below her. "And here is your deadly devil on the ground."

Thane pushed Myles off him. "Is it wearing off at all? That lightheadedness?"

Aini nodded and sure enough the hum between her eyes faded and she began a slow descent to the floor. "Your timing was spot on. So if I need to stay afloat longer, should I take two at a time?"

"We can try that out if you're up for it."

"Of course I am," she said. "I am definitely up for it," she added in a louder voice to cover the tremble in her words.

Thane pulled her into his arms. His back muscles moved under her hands and she breathed him in, loving his familiar cotton scent and the newer sage that permeated his skin beneath the slight aura of blue.

"I wish we could stay here," she said.

She hated how wistful she sounded, but the idea of being here with Thane in the lab, Father, unhurt and well fed, downstairs helping the Dionadair, and Myles, Neve, and Bran to keep them company, it was just so wonderfully...safe. Neve's mother and brothers had been moved to another Dionadair house with the code name Potato Casserole. No one here knew the location so if they were caught, they couldn't expose her family's whereabouts. It was all so much better than what Aini had imagined their situation would be at this point. She'd thought they'd all be dead in the street by now or crowding one of the king's prisons. Everyone was safely tucked away and very much alive.

But none of this was even close to being permanent.

They'd defeated Nathair's meathead thug—Thane's cousin Rodric—but there would be retribution once Nathair realized no one from the operation on Bass Rock was answering his calls because they were either dead or had gone to the rebels' side— though Thane and Bran were the only two who'd done that. This small pocket of time when Nathair didn't know what had actually happened on the island wouldn't last. Owen and his Dionadair rebels had to figure out what to do and act quickly. Everyone felt the pressure. Everyone had a guess on how Nathair would strike back and when. None of it was pleasant.

"We really need to get moving, though. I don't understand why it's taking Owen so long to come up with a plan."

"He did almost die." Myles pursed his lips. "That gives him at least two days to sit around and do jack, doesn't it?"

"We don't have two days. It's been one and a half already. The Dionadair need a plan. I mean, what are we even doing right now?" She looked at the window again.

"One day at a time, hen," Thane said. "You can't plan this. Not fully anyway."

She frowned up at him.

Myles laughed and greased a baking sheet with an oiled brush. "That is not Aini's M.O. and you know it, man. Players are going to play. Planners are going to plan. No matter how much they stress themselves in the process."

Thane held up the thermometer. "It's go time. For the candy."

"I'm not planning this part of our adventure," Aini said to Myles as she squeezed the dye bottle. Two drops fell into the sugary bubbles and spread like octopus tentacles. "Owen is going to get better and he'll have a plan that will work. The two Dionadair that went to Edinburgh and the other one that went south will be back within hours. They'll have information about Nathair and where kingsmen have been stationed and what the word is around. Owen is going to lead this. Not me."

"We'll all need to give our suggestions on how to proceed," Thane said. "That's the only way we'll find a way out of this alive. God knows just because I'm the Heir doesn't mean I know what to do."

"You've helped the Campbells plan for years. You do know military strategy," Aini argued. "Plus you're a Dreamer. I don't think it's farfetched to think you'll Dream up something we need to know along the way."

"I don't know. Last night I did Dream about an ice storm. It gave me a headache like the recurring stone Dream I had until we went to Bass Rock. But how does a Dream about a storm help? I don't even know where the rough weather will take place."

"It could be important though. We should tell Owen."

He shrugged. "As for the work I've done over the years...a full-scale rebellion isn't anything like rounding up pockets of criminals or spying on traitors." His gaze lingered on the pale scar marring the back of his hand. "We need allies."

Myles tossed the pizza cutter and scissors they'd used to cut the candy onto the countertop. Uncapping a marker, he began drawing swirling lines on his trousers. "Vera said she had ideas to talk about."

"That woman is crazy," Aini said.

Thane chuckled. "You're not wrong." He added a single teaspoon of the lavender-grape flavoring and two full table-spoons of the boosted anti-gravity concoction he and Father had come up with. "I don't think this will kill anyone," he said, eyeing the candy, "but whoever eats these will not feel normal for a good hour or more after the effects wear off. Not to mention how bizarre they'll feel during the experience." A loose curl of dark blond hair fell over one eye as he muttered some-thing about hormones and adrenaline, then rattled off a formula interspersed with strings of Scots Gaelic.

Rain began to fall against the roof and its metallic scent permeated the room. The smell reminded Aini of blood, of the night on Bass Rock Island where she'd thought she was going to lose everyone. An unseen pull tugged her fingers away from the pot's covered handle and onto Thane's forearm. She brushed her thumb over his skin and soaked in his warmth, the solidity of his presence. He was the true Heir to the Scottish throne, the one meant to free their homeland from the hands of the tyrant English king, but he was also the one who made her heart whole. He belonged to everyone. But he was also *just hers*.

His big hand covered her fingers and he smiled, though his eyes darkened. "Do you think they'll follow me?"

He was talking about the clan chieftains. At some point very soon, Aini, Myles, Neve, Vera, and several other Dionadair rebels would have to travel to Thane's massive estate in Inveraray to meet with the men and women who influenced the bulk of Scotland's people and, most importantly, its weapons. It'd be a huge meeting of all the clans loyal to the Campbells and the vast majority of Campbells themselves. Thane and Aini would have to convince them that Thane should lead the clans instead of Nathair. Then there was the little bit about a full-on rebellion against the king.

Aini poured the hot, colored sugar mix onto the baking sheet. "I'm not saying it'll be easy to persuade the clans, but surely when they've heard what really happened to Rodric..." She fought a shiver remembering how the ghost kings engulfed him and the others. "And how the stone roared for you, they'll come around."

To say the least. No one would want that curse on their head. Vague folklore said the Coronation Stone's curse promised *the power of the old to protect their own*. On Bass Rock, the power had shown up in the form of the dead rulers of Scotland supernaturally killing Thane's horrible cousin Rodric and the other Campbells there. Aini wasn't sure how the curse would work if another enemy threatened Thane. Even Neve with her substantial knowledge of legend and history didn't know the true nature of the stone's curse.

"After all, you're a Campbell too," Aini said. "And a more powerful one. Or, you will be. I mean. Come on. Nathair doesn't have the spirits of old kings on his side."

"He has a huge army. And the very-much-alive king's army too. And these clansmen, they've been trained to follow Nathair. To fall in line. To support his agenda and my grandfather's for generations. When someone has been brainwashed, it's nearly impossible to persuade them of anything that contradicts what they've been taught. Look at what I've done in my life. But I'm no fool. And I do have a soul. A heart. Despite that, I did as I was told almost every time Nathair asked me to do unspeakable things. Years spent by the fire and at clan gatherings, reciting Campbell oaths and lies...breaking through that conditioning... it's an impossible task we have, my Seer."

He said that last word a little wryly. The Dionadair had fallen into the habit of calling Aini "their Seer" lately and it felt uncomfortable at best. Wrong on some days. She did See memories implanted on items that were important sentimentally to others. She also had the sixth sense they called Ghost Talking. She'd commanded the ghost kings to protect Thane on Bass Rock. But she had no idea how to call up ghosts when they might need them, if Nathair attacked suddenly.

"The clans that support Clan Campbell, and Clan Campbell itself, they must realize they're being misled," Aini said. "Mistreated. The king has shown more and more that he hates and fears the Scots. With the marriage laws. The taxes. The firing squad deaths after only the pretense of a trial. He's taking our people and executing them as he sees fit. And Nathair is at the head of it. I'm sure some of them have lost loved ones to the prisons or the firing squads. There have to be sixth-sensers within their ranks. We can convince them. Surely, just the fact that they aren't permitted to wear tartan unless they're in Clan Campbell should show clearly enough that Nathair doesn't respect the other clans."

"Most will be Campbells." Sadness drew Thane's voice down a few notes.

Aini touched his shoulder, feeling the muscle and bone beneath his shirt. "We just need a real plan. Owen has to come around. His color looked better today. He'll be fine soon, right?"

He had to be. Vera could not run this operation, and despite what the others claimed, Aini couldn't either. She was completely unqualified. The rest of the rebels were so used to Owen running things that none had come forward to suggest a plan either.

Aini's father jogged up the stairs, a wrinkled paper in his hands. His clothes were ironed to perfection despite the multiple threats going on in the world around them. He'd shaved too. The line around his tidy beard was sharp as the edge of a candy cutter. Aini approved.

He held up the paper and eyed everyone. "I have a very wild idea, my dears."

Myles's eyebrows lifted. "Okay..."

Aini peered over his shoulder to read the words inked onto the paper. "What is it?"

"Well, it appears to be a grocery list," he said. "But I don't think it is."

Thane looked up from the candy, his eyes narrowed with intense focus.

"Do share," Myles said, standing next to Aini. "Wild ideas are probably good for a rebellion."

"Agreed," Aini said.

Her father shook the paper out and studied it. "You see the odd use of a single letter for people's names?"

"They've just abbreviated family members though, aye?" Thane had made his way over.

"I don't think so. It fits too well. Think about the leaders of the French forces in the Channel."

"Um, I honestly can't say that I've been paying enough attention. Been busy, you know." Aini raised an eyebrow.

He replicated the gesture. "Of course. But I heard the Weekly Address while in captivity."

Just the mention of Father's time spent in the hands of the Campbells made the room sway in front of Aini's eyes. It had been the worst time in her life. And when she'd seen his finger on the ground after that fight at the barn...

"You all right?" Thane had come around and was now circling her waist with an arm to steady her.

She welcomed the support. "Yes. I'm fine. Sorry, Father. Go on."

He nodded smartly though she could tell he was worried about her. "Seven names came up frequently in the reports about the last clash with the French off the coast. I rejoiced in every mention of them because they're truly giving King John some real trouble. He deserves some trouble, wouldn't you agree?"

"That's one way of putting it," Aini said.

The murdering king deserved more than trouble. He deserved death for all the sixth-sensers he'd ordered killed, those he'd starved through higher taxes, the couples he'd torn apart simply because one was Scottish and didn't have his approval, and most of all, for the children orphaned and left in the streets when their parents never returned from what he and Nathair called *questioning*. Once those poor souls were in the famed cells under Edinburgh, waiting to be questioned, they were lost to their families. Aini had only been without Father for a short time. She couldn't imagine worrying and waiting for years upon years. It was the worst kind of torture and no one should have to suffer it, let alone sweet little children.

Father ran his finger down the list. "Well, of those military leaders named, one begins with a B, one with a C, and another with an A. All those letters are shown here."

Aini read the list to herself.

B's milk

C's big box of oaties

two dozen eggs for C too

A's bag of apples even if they're a bit overripe

"Or it could just be a list of groceries, Mr. MacGregor," Myles said, shrugging.

"You may be right, Myles. But I think it is at least worth looking into because of its source."

"Did you find it?" Thane asked.

"No. Rob did. One of the Dionadair. The one with the cap?"

"I like him." Myles smiled. "He made me a great cheese sandwich this morning and told me two dirty jokes I'd never heard."

Aini smacked Myles. "Focus."

A grin flickered over Thane's full lips.

Father cleared his throat. "Rob found it in the house of a prominent banker who the Dionadair suspect is the contact for an English operative in France."

"You should've led with that." Myles elbowed Father gently.

He laughed. "It's not like I'm Dionadair. I don't know how these things work."

"So what does this mean in your humble opinion?" Aini asked.

"I think it's a report on the number of ships outside Calais, near the disputed territory. I believe these are the ships

England's forces will come up against during their next attack. B is Beauchamp, that artillery expert they dug up from Provence. He was in the Weekly Address, remember? C is General Caron. He has a flyer carrier out there and his entire fleet of fighters."

"And A must be that Captain Abbe," Aini said. "Even I've heard of him."

"Oh!" Myles slapped his leg. "That's the old man with the fleet of sailors from the last colonial war. We colonials love that guy."

"He saved your arses when the king decided he wanted half the cut on exports, right?" Thane handed the list back to Father. "Made reducing that tax a part of the peace treaty."

"Yep. The leader of Mint has a tattoo of him."

Mint was Myles's favorite band. Aini thought perhaps they overused the banjo a little. "What an honor." She handed the list back to Father. "Did you tell Owen yet?"

"Owen's not in his right mind, squirrel." Father's eyes were kind, but Aini didn't want to hear that news.

"Are you coming with us when we go to Inveraray? You can change your mind. You don't have to stay here."

"If you truly need me there, I will go. You know I will. But I don't think having an old man with you is a good idea. You need fighters. I'd only be in your way."

Aini pulled him into a hug. "You are never in my way."

"And you're not old," Thane added.

Father smoothed the hair at the back of Aini's head and she breathed in the wool scent of his sweater. "I'm off to talk to Rob," he said. "He and Samantha will have thoughts on what to do with this information. I'm also hoping I can make contact with Darnwell. The king is keeping a very close eye on him and his wife, I'm sure. But maybe they can help us somehow."

Lord Darnwell was an eccentric noble—his mustache was

phenomenal—who just happened to be married to the French queen's half-sister. He and Father had bonded over how to operate Enliven. Darnwell had his own boutique business. He painted miniature portraits. Most of the nobility looked down on his quirky art, but Father had, rightly so, appreciated the man's unique talent. Aini herself had danced with the lord at several elite parties over the years. Contacting him, well, who knew what kind of situation he was in with the war in France? To think that he might be able to somehow help them, that was surely a long shot.

"You're sure making contact won't put him and us in danger?" Aini asked.

"I will get the Dionadair to help me use a code. I'll only go forward with it if Owen agrees to it." And with a sad smile, Father left the makeshift lab.

Aini's heart warred with itself. She wanted Father with her through this nightmare, but she also needed him to be safe. He'd been through so much. Having him out of the direct line of fire was also a necessity to her mental health.

Myles switched on the television. A man in a sharp, blue suit stood in front of two cages that each held a sixth-senser. Aini shivered. Their hair was matted and bruises colored their cheekbones and arms. The kingsmen had gagged the sixth-sensers. The king was still so afraid of what they'd say. They'd been *questioned*, the reporter said. Aini shook her head. Not questioned. They'd been tortured. She couldn't wait until the slimy king found out he wasn't going to be able to hold Scotland in his vicious hands for much longer.

Myles cut the finished hard candies while Aini worked on another batch. Thane set a plastic tray of finished taffy on the end of the counter. Inside, golden strips of sugar and Cone5, wrapped in pale wax paper, sat ready for the experiments they'd planned.

If things went well with Thane's mother and the clans in Inveraray, the team would run the tests at the estate.

If things at Inveraray went badly, and the clan decided not to believe Aini and Thane's story and came to the conclusion more sixth-senser blood should be spilled right then and there, well, there wouldn't be any call for altered sweets or battle plans. The rebellion would be over before it started.

So many lives hung in the balance.

As Aini stirred the second batch of hard candy, the pink-lavender hue in the pot darkened into a deep purple, like circles under tired eyes. "I added too much dye. These look awful."

Myles peered over her shoulder, smelling faintly like the white pepper and nutmeg chewing gum he'd munched on this morning during his quest to fool his eyes into seeing some version of the Loch Ness monster. He wouldn't listen when Neve told him this wasn't even close to the right area for that story.

"The color is fine," Myles said. "A little depressing maybe, but maybe since it's darker, we'll remember how much more powerful it is."

Breathing out through her nose, Aini took the candy from the heat and poured it out on the baking sheet. She locked eyes with Thane who was cleaning the taffy puller with a wet rag. "Will you two finish up here? I'm going to see Owen."

Thane met her at the door. His shirt collar was nearly worn through. It hung loosely to one side, showing off his collarbone and the spot where not so long ago his Campbell necklace hung.

"Do you want me to come with you?" he asked.

He cleaned taffy from his fingers and Aini couldn't help but remember the time they'd kissed in the middle of making the candy. Sugar, sparkling colors, the heat of his body against hers...

"Aini?"

"What? Oh no, that's okay. If it's important, I'll grab you and the others."

"All right then."

He went back to his work, stoic as ever. She smiled at his broad back, then trotted down the stairs. She wished they had time to have fun together. But every minute the Dionadair waited to act was another minute Nathair might find out what happened and move to get the king to help him crush the burgeoning rebellion. There wasn't any time to lose.

Through damp, browning grass dotted with purple mushrooms, Aini hurried to the main house. She would tidy up this situation and get things moving. She didn't want to plan their next move, but she was more than fine with putting a fire under those who did know how to take down a monster.

CHAPTER 2
EXPERIMENTS AND FEAR

Thane grabbed the box of caramels he'd made before everyone woke up this morning, said bye to Myles, and slipped out the safe house's back door. Wind bumped against his cheeks and pressed into his glasses. It was colder than it should've been for this early in the autumn. Behind the house where they'd been since their quick escape from Edinburgh, steep hills sloped into a narrow stretch of tall, yellow grass and moss-covered rock.

The box lid slid off easily and the smell of caramel wafted into the crisp air. The others might think of him as the Heir or some great genius, but Thane knew well he'd made plenty of mistakes. This candy might end up being one of his most embarrassing ones. Better to test it outside, away from everyone. Safer too. That first batch had developed a nasty slime and he hadn't wanted anyone to touch it let alone test the stuff. This batch looked fine, but he really didn't know. Who knew what this blend of blood and muscle altering chemicals would do? He didn't want to accidentally explode all over everyone in the guest house.

With a deep breath, he bit off a corner of one caramel. It was delicious. At least that part was right. Despite what was coming, what he had to do very soon, he really hoped this altered sweet didn't drop him dead where he stood.

A slow heat rose from his heart and into his throat. He touched his cheeks as they flushed hot. His quadriceps spasmed. It wasn't painful, but it felt very odd. He swallowed. He really, really didn't want to die. He wanted to enjoy at least one more day with Aini.

Muscle spasms squeezed their way down his body. Trapezius. Rhomboids. Obliques. The tendons around his groin even tightened.

"Whoa. Take it easy," he mumbled to himself, extremely glad he'd made the decision to do this away from prying eyes.

Then his body seemed to settle into a low hum of tension and heat. Like he was a car idling, ready to take off fast from the line and leave the rest of the traffic behind.

"That's much better."

With a grin, he started to run.

Wind sheared over his face as the surrounding hills blurred to each side. He hurtled easily over a boulder coated in orange moss and veered left to avoid a patch of black mud.

It felt amazing.

Struggling to keep up with his muscles, his lungs burned hot as his blood. He was almost flying, his long stride eating up the distance between the house and the end of the valley. Peeking over his shoulder, he saw the roof and the sturdy walls—now just a spot on the horizon.

He threw his head back and laughed out loud. "This is madness!"

Turning quickly, he ran back toward the house, his legs moving too quickly for him to see properly. His lungs shook inside his chest, and he slowed, legs humming still. Back where he'd started, he put his hands on his knees and gulped the cold air.

When he straightened, five faces appeared in the back windows. Dionadair. Their mouths hung open. They looked at him like he was a god.

He snatched up the box of caramels and held it high. "It was just the candy. Anyone could do it."

But they either couldn't understand what his actions meant or they refused to believe he was any less than what they wanted him to be because they kept staring and raised crossed thumbs high as a sign of respect.

Thane shook his head and tucked the caramels under his arm. He almost wished he thought of himself as highly as they did. Maybe then he'd be as confident about claiming the roles of Clan Campbell chief and King of Scotland as they were about the whole mad thing.

He thought of the storm Dream he'd had last night, the feel of the ice on his skin, the sound of the wind against a car window...

Yes, he knew being a Dreamer and the Heir was in his blood. Yes, he knew the prophecy and the ghost kings all proved he and Aini were meant to do all of this. But a big, fat chunk of him still couldn't accept it. He knew his own limitations. He was only twenty-years-old, for God's sake. He didn't have the life experience of someone like Lewis MacGregor or half the Dionadair.

Thane knew Aini could play her role. She'd been bossing people about for years. She had the very soul of a leader, the practicality of a general, and the ability to learn very quickly what she needed to know to lead the Dionadair.

But Thane, he'd never wanted to lead. He'd longed to leave Clan Campbell, not rule it. He did love Scotland though. To his core. It was his breath and his heart. He only prayed he wouldn't destroy it trying to live up to the prophecy that tied him to this green and lovely land.

He decided to try one more run to see how long the caramels lasted. Taking off toward the valley again, he recited the Periodic Table to calm his nerves. ...N, Nitrogen...

A sudden memory of his father's face blinked through his brain.

Nathair was smiling and it was terrible like it had always been.

"No!" Thane sped up though the caramel's effect was wearing off. "I am no longer a Campbell like you. I will fight you. I will fight your influence."

His legs stretched to jump over a shining puddle of rainwater. The silver surface flashed the reflection of an angry man who looked far too much like Nathair Campbell, despite the different coloring. Thane dragged himself to an abrupt halt. He fisted his hands and let the bones of his knuckles painfully strain against his skin. The world tilted a bit. Taking a breath, Thane threw his head back and shouted into the wilderness. Another breath and he'd purged some of his fear and rage.

He brought the memory of Nathair's smile to mind. "I will not be like you. I will never hurt those who love me. I am not your son. I am not your son. I am not your son."

If he said it enough, he hoped he'd begin to believe it.

Thane could only allow himself to rule the country he loved if he completely and totally broke away from his father and turned the meaning of the name Campbell into something else entirely. Children could not go around afraid of the name. Women could not worry about their intuition, praying it was not some latent sixth sense surfacing. Men could not lie awake at night and wonder if a Campbell would be coming for them in the morning.

Campbell had to become a name the people loved.

"I am Thane Campbell. First of the new line of kings. Thane Campbell, named by the Coronation Stone, paired with Macbeth's Seer, and fated to help Scotland break free and rise up."

Suddenly bashful, he spun to make sure no one had followed him. Only a small bird hopped from a wide fern to a mossy rock. It chirped lightly at him.

"I am Thane Campbell and I'm a fool." He rubbed his face harshly, shoving his glasses into his wind-tangled hair.

When he turned toward the house, he saw Myles coming out and heading toward the caramels.

"You shouldn't eat those!" Thane gestured toward the box. "You just had the gum this morning!" It might be too much for his system or even for his brain.

Myles obviously didn't hear because he lifted the box lid and popped one into his mouth. Waving a hand, Myles chewed while Thane began the run back. When Thane was still a stone's throw from the house, Myles leaned forward to boak his treat all over the unsuspecting grass. The Dionadair who'd cheered Thane on were still at the window. One pointed and another laughed.

Myles, always a good sport, wiped his mouth with his sleeve then bowed to his audience.

"I tried to stop you." Thane put a hand on Myles's shoulder. "Why don't you have a seat? I'll fetch some water. You shouldn't mix altered sweets."

"I hadn't had anything for over two hours."

"This is all experimental. I really don't think it's a good idea to eat more than one type of candy in forty-eight hours. You must metabolize through one—"

Myles held up a hand. "Got it. Got it. Only one type of yummy at a time or you spill your breakfast all over granny's petunias."

"Oh I don't think it would merely be vomiting if you'd eaten them closer together."

Myles's frown deepened. "So like..." He held his hands near his temples. "Kaboom?"

"Aye. Maybe. Probably less dramatic but just as deadly. Seizures. Cardiac arrest. Something of that sort as a first step toward the grave."

"You are kind of a poet."

Thane glared.

"No, really. That was like a song lyric. First step toward the grave..." He began humming.

Thane assumed he wouldn't boak again, so he started to leave, but Myles grabbed his sleeve.

"Hey, I need some advice, man," Myles said. "I love my mother like a snowman loves summer, but I'm thinking she should at least know some of what's going on over here with me."

Myles's mother ran a cotton plantation in the southern colonies. From what Thane had heard, she was a horrible woman who paid her workers very little. She acted like some sort of queen in her remote corner of the world. Had loads of money, for certain.

"You'd have to be very careful."

"No kidding."

"I just mean...she may want to get involved."

"To save me? Yeah, no. She won't. That won't be a problem."

Thane put a hand on Myles's shoulder. "Sorry she's like that, pal."

"I'm used to it," Myles said, but the pain in his eyes told another tale. "I just don't want her trying to contact me at the townhouse and screwing something up."

"Aye. Well, get with Lewis and the others. See if you can come up with a coded message to send to her via a safe phone. Just to tell her there has been trouble, but you're fine."

"For now. Should I mention I might be dead soon?"

Thane laughed without humor. "Might want to leave that bit off."

Myles saluted him. "Thanks for listening, Master of the Universe."

Thane rolled his eyes. "No problem." He clapped him on the back and went inside to find Aini. He needed someone sane to talk to, and that someone was neither himself nor Myles.

CHAPTER 3
TO LIGHT THE FUSE

Bran spread the materials for a low explosive and a high explosive on the table by the safe house's garden shed. He ran a careful hand over the complicated high-end detonators he'd nicked from the Campbell stores before Bass Rock. They'd been hidden in the lining of his coat and he wasn't sorry at all for taking them. They were tricky buggers to make and having a good example to study would help Bran's assistants craft more just like them to use against their enemies. A sealed, small barrel of gunpowder sat at the end of the table. He hoped they wouldn't have to travel with it, but he had a sneaking suspicion they would.

The sound of boots on fallen leaves crunched behind him and he turned to see the three Dionadair that had agreed to work with him on the explosives side of this rebellion. All three were skinny malinky longlegs, to be sure. Their limbs were like saplings gnawed bare by overzealous wildlife, all pale and straight beneath their shirtsleeves. Despite their less than hearty bodies, the lads' eyes held fire, and that was the most important thing.

To deal with this kind of thing, they had to have a pretty serious helping of courage inside them.

"All right then, my men. Study what I've gathered here. This is what a deconstructed low explosive looks like. This kind are set up to burn. They won't blast unless tightly cooped up in a proper container. This here is an example of a high explosive. These must have a detonator and will explode like the world is coming apart. This is very similar to what the Campbells used at your rebel barn the night they nearly offed their own leader, the idiots." He pointed to the detonator. "I need help constructing a few more of these. I'd like to have four fully functional high explosives on hand when we head out of here to God knows where. Then, depending on what plan our leaders decide on, you three can make more and send them to where the fighting takes place. That's not for us to worry about now, though. Our part of this is simply to get the explosives prepped. Do you understand? Any questions?"

"Aye. My brothers and I have all made explosives. We know what you're wanting." The tallest of them touched the detonator with finger and thumb. "What we'd like to know is why you're in charge of this team and not the other way around?"

Bran wasn't sure if he meant brothers as in blood kin or brothers as in brothers in arms. Regardless, they seemed to be of one mind as they stared him down. But Bran knew exactly how to deal with passionate folk dedicated to a cause. He'd had enough dealings with that to last a lifetime.

"I'm leading this group because your Seer and your Heir told me to do so, may they rise together." He held up his hands and crossed his thumbs over his head.

The lads nodded and copied his gesture. The distrust in their faces faded. "Let's get to work then," the tallest said.

Side by side, they twisted metal, tucked components into

their proper spots, and used pliers to make adjustments. The men did well, Bran thought. They were moving carefully, slowly, methodically, and keeping a good eye on that gunpowder, showing it the respect it deserved.

When they had the four completed explosives ready, Bran shifted them into a straw-lined wooden crate. One of the lads fit the top onto the crate and together they pushed it tightly closed. Bran dusted his hands and surveyed his team.

"If we get the call to head out into this madness as a group, good. If we don't, and the opportunity to join me later arises, please speak up to your elders and do come find me. I trust you now and I hope you trust me too. I'd rather not work with this stuff around strangers. Do you agree?"

They nodded and Bran worried for a moment whether their skinny necks were up to the job of holding their heads on.

"It wouldn't hurt for you to eat more and...do some pushups, for God's sake. You're too thin, all of you."

Bran took the long way around to enter the safe house through the kitchen door, his mind throwing out scenarios as he walked over gravel and grass.

Where exactly was Nathair now and what was the man up to? Nathair had lost his core unit, the men he trusted to do the jobs he considered highest priority. If he knew what had happened on Bass Rock, if he knew they were dead and gone, he'd build a new group, wouldn't he?

The man had a knack for finding those who would follow him into the fire. The poor, the desperate, but the rich too. He had a way of persuading everyone within earshot that he had the truth of things and knew the way the world should be.

Thane had always fought it. Bran had seen the fight in Thane's eyes a thousand times, that look he had when Nathair raged on about how the Campbells were God's gift to the world.

Bran seemed to have an antidote to Nathair's rhetoric flowing in his veins. He was the only one Thane used to confide in and he alone spoke up in agreement with Thane's tentative, early arguments with Nathair. It's why Bran had stayed by Thane's side. He wanted to be there for him always. The battle Thane fought, mentally and quite often physically, against his father was one no man should have to fight alone.

Bran pushed the safe house's kitchen door open with more force than he'd intended and the white wood banged against the frame, startling a Dionadair in an apron.

"Sorry," he mumbled, slipping out of the haze of cooking smoke and the scent of butter, into the low light of the main house.

If Nathair did have a new core unit of operatives, they would be fearsome to be sure. Nathair wouldn't play around with the possibility that more kin would go to Thane's side of things. Nathair's new men would be even more ruthless, if that was possible. They'd be cold and professional.

A shiver ran over Bran as he closed himself into his small bedroom to think. The bed creaked under his weight and he put his head in his hands, remembering Bass Rock island—the ghosts and the wind, the roar and the truth.

"I hope it's enough," he said to the empty room. "Or we're all good as dead where we stand."

CHAPTER 4
SLEEPING LEADER

The stairs leading to the room where Owen slept zigzagged like a mountain trail. With every step, Aini practiced what she would say to rouse the head of the Dionadair rebels. Surely she could help him shake off the lingering stupor from the blood loss he suffered and put his mind to the task of the rebellion. This was Owen Bethune after all—owlish, practical, a cutthroat in herringbone—and this was the moment he'd been waiting for, working toward his entire life. He would know what to do next. The job of organizing rebels and supplies and attacks didn't have to fall onto Aini's and Thane's shoulders.

She would ask him how he was feeling. Tell him about the candy they'd crafted. Inform him that she and Thane were ready to follow his orders and work as a team to defeat Nathair and, eventually, the king. His people needed him and his experience, his passion. Now was the time. He'd rise up out of bed, face flushed with resolve, and lead them to the future they were all hoping for. A future with the true Heir on the throne, Scotland as its own master, and freedom for all, including every single sixth-senser that chose to make this green land their home.

Dodie, Vera's ox-like brother, stood guard outside Owen's room. He gave Aini a respectful nod and mumbled, "Morning, Seer," as she passed.

Pale yellow light soaked through Owen's closed curtains and into the rumpled duvet. The sun illuminated the blue half-moons under the rebel leader's eyes and the new wrinkles spanning his temples. Aini smoothed the blankets and pulled a straight-backed wooden chair beside the bed. She folded her hands in her lap and cleared her throat.

Owen's eyes opened. "Seer."

"How are you feeling?"

He ran a knuckle over the red stubble on his chin and reached for a glass of water on the nightstand.

Aini grabbed it and helped him take a drink. "Your informants should return soon. We need to know what your plans are."

His eyes shuttered closed. "Ask Vera," he mumbled.

Setting the glass back very carefully, Aini took a breath. "Vera isn't you. We need you to lay out a plan."

"I can't."

"You can."

"My mind...I'm still...foggy."

Behind a tower of clean, folded cloth, a man bustled in. "Our leader needs his rest, Seer. Please." He began unwrapping Owen's wound with sharp movements.

"Fine. You can rest, Owen. But first, just tell me how we can approach the clans and get their support. Do you have any thoughts on that? And what should we have them do if we manage to talk them into joining us?"

Owen's eyelids fluttered shut and he turned toward the nurse.

"With all respect, Seer, you must leave now," the nurse said.

"This is the revolution you and your family have struggled toward." Aini gripped Owen's sleeve. "Now is your moment. Just tell me what to do and I'll do it. Please."

The nurse stood. "Seer. You'll never get anything from the man if he has no time to recover."

Aini sighed, deflating.

The nurse shooed her out of the room with a nod and expectant eyes.

Shaking her head, she left as ordered. She didn't want to hurt Owen, to keep him from healing properly, but surely he could still think up some strategy that would get Thane and her to Inveraray without trouble. Or tell them to do something she hadn't even thought of, like go to another town and use part of the rebel network to contact some of the chieftains. There were countless ideas he might give them if he only had the will.

"Now Seer, it's not polite to snarl at sick men." Vera sashayed around the corner and put a hand on her hip. "I hear you don't trust my guidance."

Aini blew out a breath. "It's not that I don't trust you. It's just that Owen is your leader. Our leader."

"No. You're right. He does have a better head for strategy. But I have a plan and you'll listen to it, won't you? Besides, Owen will be up and well soon and then you can side with him against me again." A sad grin passed over her mouth. "Ready to hear my thoughts?"

"Of course." Aini was pretty certain this plan would involve maiming multiple people for no apparent reason and driving like madmen into a line of Campbells armed with nothing more than a bludgeon and some attitude.

"We head out at night once we hear Nathair is gone from the area along with his best men. Travel quick—"

Aini crossed her arms. "And arrive at the gates of Inveraray like bandits begging to be shot on site?"

"We'd stop first and clean up. We'd make a fine entrance." Vera raised her chin.

"In the middle of the night."

Vera spread her arms wide. "Then we send word first."

"To whom?"

"Thane's mother."

That wasn't a bad idea. "I'll talk to Thane about discussing this with his mother and what he thinks the risks may be to her and us. You go talk to your brother. You know as well as I do that we need his brain."

"Aye. I can't argue that." Vera gave Aini a respectful nod before heading into Owen's room.

The door swung shut, and Aini stared at the clear plastic knob. She didn't want to wrap Thane's mother into this before they had a solid idea of what they were going to do and when. The heating vents switched on and blew Aini's hair across her face as she walked downstairs. Gritting her teeth, she tucked the wayward strands of her unruly mane behind her ears. Her mind was full to bursting. Owen simply had to snap out of this.

In the small guest room she shared with Neve, Aini slid the top drawer of the sleek, modern dresser open. Two rows of tiny glass jars clinked together lightly, their green lids labeled in clear white letters. She grabbed up the rosemary, basil, juniper berry, peppermint, and clary sage. With the lids unscrewed, she took a small spoonful of each and shifted the ingredients into her mortar's smooth, marble interior. She twisted and pressed down with the pestle and the sharp scents of the concoction filled the room.

"If this doesn't wake Owen up," she mumbled to herself, "and get him planning for us, nothing will."

"What are you up to?" Neve appeared at the door with a wooden spoon coated in melted chocolate. She licked the back and cocked her head at Aini.

"We're headed into war, real war, and you're eating chocolate?"

"I'd say that's the best time to eat chocolate. A person needs comfort now more than ever."

A smile broke over Aini's mouth despite her worries' attempt to drag the corners of her lips into a frown. "I love you, Neve."

"Back at you, darling." Neve offered the coated spoon.

Aini waved it off. "I'm making a little something to rouse our Owen."

Neve sniffed at the mortar, then jumped back. "That would rouse my dead great aunt."

Aini set the mortar down and dusted the dried rosemary off her hands. "Then it must be ready."

CONCOCTION IN HAND, AINI HEADED BACK TOWARD OWEN'S room. Dodie was gone and a new guard had replaced him. He didn't say a word to Aini or Neve when they opened the door. Thankfully, the nurse wasn't there, but Vera was drawing a fresh sheet up to Owen's chin. Aini settled herself on the bed's opposite side, beside the nightstand.

"What a smell!" Vera's nose wrinkled at Aini's concoction.

Aini scooped a portion and began to shift it into Owen's untouched soup.

Vera reached across her brother and pushed the mortar away from the bowl. Herbs scattered over the small table. "You're not feeding my brother that stinking mess."

The guard at the door sucked a breath and leaned in to see what would make someone talk to the Seer that way.

"I mean," Vera said, schooling her tone, "I don't think it'll help, Seer." She fluttered her lashes, obviously trying to look young and penitent and failing miserably.

Aini rolled her eyes. "It might. And it won't hurt him regardless."

She dabbed a bit of the mix into a spoonful of yellow soup and nodded to Neve who put an arm behind Owen to help him sit up. His eyes remained closed.

"Owen. We have something that'll make you feel better." She set the spoon against his lips.

He took a sip, then spat it back out, eyes flashing open. Groaning, he pushed the spoon away and spilled the rest of the portion on the blankets and Aini's arm. "I don't want to feel better."

Aini froze, her gaze on Vera. Vera touched her lips, her face pale.

"What do you mean, brother? We're on the verge of what we've been fighting for our whole lives." She sat, making the bed dip a little as she reached over him and ran a hand over his cheek. "This is the rebellion. It's actually happening. Of course you want to mend so you can help in the fight. Our Seer is here. She is ready to lead."

Aini put a hand to her suddenly throbbing head. This was not going the way she'd planned. They could not run this revolution without its leader.

Owen rolled onto his stomach and pressed his face into his pillow. "My mind...I can't..."

Vera stood.

The nurse pushed into the room. "Seer, with all due respect, this man suffered extreme blood loss and is fighting temporary memory loss and what I'm sure is a crippling mental fog." He sniffed the air. "While I appreciate your knowledge of natural remedies and do support their use, know that our leader will continue to heal in his own time and we must make adjustments as needed. Now, please consider my advice and let him rest."

He didn't have to yell. Something squirmed in Aini's chest. "I'm sorry. You're right."

A strangled sound crawled out of Owen's mouth. Aini spun to see him thrashing on the bed.

Vera pinned his arms down.

"No!" The nurse put a hand on Vera's arm. "Back away. Give him space. He will get through this, but he needs space."

Owen kept seizing. Aini went cold all over.

"What is wrong with him?" Vera's hands went to her mouth.

"It's a seizure. He had one two hours ago. It is normal with as much blood loss as he experienced," the nurse said.

Owen finally settled and Vera's hands went to her sides.

The nurse held a hand toward the door. "Now, please leave him alone for a while. I'll be here the entire time. I promise."

The hallway outside Owen's room was too quiet. Neve, Aini, and Vera just stood and stared at one another.

A girl who looked a little younger than Aini pounded up the stairs, cheeks bright red. "The informants returned, Seer. None of them managed to get a 100 percent solid take on Nathair Campbell's current location or where he may be heading. Nothing conclusive."

Vera whispered a curse.

The girl continued. "One scout did overhear a report on a kingsman radio frequency that stated the earl was seen at an Edinburgh judge's house, but that information is sketchy at best seeing as the reporter didn't specifically mention Nathair's name."

Aini rolled her mother's ring around her finger. Hmm. They really needed to know if Nathair was nearby. Everything hinged on that information.

Neve bit her lower lip. "We can't wait around forever though, right? He'll be coming after us sooner rather than later."

"Tell us what you want us to do, Seer." Vera clasped her hands and swallowed. "Some of the elder members will want to meet, to hear what you have to say." She glanced at the door to Owen's room. "You and Thane."

Aini spun and rubbed her temples. This was all moving too quickly. She didn't know what to do. "Why do you want me to lead you? Let the elder members lead."

Vera grabbed Aini's arm in a viselike grip. "Why do we want you to lead?! Because you're the Seer, woman! The prophecy called you. You are the entire reason for the existence of the Dionadair. You are Macbeth's Seer and I knew you would come to us and take us into a world where Scotland is free. You are born to this. Don't doubt it." Her eyes were wild and a strand of her dark hair had fallen over one cheek. "They will only follow you. I love my brother and I hope he comes around to help, but you are who we need. Who we must have. It is destined. This is fate."

"Should we talk?" Thane said from the bottom of the staircase, his face full of concern. Sun streamed through the front windows and shone across his light hair and the corners of his glasses. Pink spots colored his cheeks like he'd been outside in the cold.

The twisting feeling in Aini's chest tightened in time with Vera's hold on her arm. Whatever she told the Dionadair to do, whatever she and Thane decided, the outcome would sit squarely on their shoulders, hers and Thane's. She didn't want the responsibility. Not like this. Not without Owen and his guidance. No matter how much this was supposed to be her fate.

She took a breath and detached Vera's claws, finger by finger. "Yes, please, Thane. That would be wonderful. Let's go ahead and get together with the Dionadair elders."

Vera jerked her chin in a quick nod and marched down the stairs. "Rob! Samantha. The rest of you lot. We're having a meeting!" She disappeared around the corner along with the girl, leaving Thane and Aini to themselves.

CHAPTER 5
FEEDING THE FIRE

At the base of the stairs, Thane cleaned his glasses with the edge of his shirt. "What did the scouts say about Nathair's whereabouts?"

"They couldn't find out anything for sure," Aini said. "They think he might be in Edinburgh."

"Should we move forward or stay until the informants gather more concrete evidence on where he is? I tried to call my mother, but she isn't answering."

"I don't know. We can ask the others and see what they think. By the way, where is Bran?"

"He'll be in soon. Right now, he is meeting with an explosives team," Thane said. Aini's fear must've shown all over her face because he quickly added, "For later. For the true battle that'll come later."

She took a shuddering breath and nodded. The war. Yes. It was going to happen whether they wanted it to or not now. "I don't want to be in charge of this," she whispered.

"Neither do I. I'm guessing not many would want this job of ours." A wry grin washed the frown from his face but didn't clear the fear from behind his eyes.

She wanted to take his hand and feel that warmth that only he had, the heat that tingled against her skin and made her feel both challenged and protected at the same time. It was a strange, perfect combination that she was quickly becoming addicted to.

With everything that was going on, they hadn't had any time alone in what felt like forever. Did he even want to hold her hand? To feel her skin on his? Maybe his head was too full of their fate and what they were trying to do. She wouldn't blame him. But it would hurt. It would hurt a lot. The twisting inside her flared into her throat and made it difficult to swallow. She moved her fingers toward his, but he was looking at the gathered Dionadair in the room down the hall and didn't notice.

Once the group—including Neve and Myles—was assembled on couches and around the floor in the living room, Aini followed Thane.

The sun bled through the red curtains, giving Neve's and Myles's faces a strange hue as they talked, heads close together. Black shadows clung to the corner beside a tall grandfather clock that ticked away the seconds they had until Nathair realized what had happened and came after them in force.

All eyes went to Aini. It didn't seem like she had much of a choice about leading. These people believed in the prophecy and the Seer and she had to fill the role or risk the rebellion falling apart and everyone dying in vain. It had to be her.

"Okay fine," she said, ignoring her jangling nerves. "We don't yet know where Nathair is, so we're going to send someone into the local kingsman's office tonight to break in and nose about.

We have to know where he is. Once we know for certain he isn't breathing down our necks, we'll move forward and a team will depart from this safe house."

"Bran can handle the kingsman's office," Thane said. "He knows how to keep from being caught, and if he is, his looks are so average that it most likely won't be an issue if Nathair has put out descriptions of us. Bran can talk his way out of a lot of things."

"He's better looking than average," Aini said. Neve and Vera nodded knowingly and Thane cocked his head. Aini shrugged. "Well, he is. But I see what you mean. Brown hair. Brown eyes. Average height. Yes. Good plan. As long as he fully agrees and is okay with the risk."

"I'll talk to him after this," Thane said.

"Once we learn where the King's Deathbringer is lurking," Vera said, "we'll leave here at night, right?" She was nodding like they'd already agreed and a few of the elder members of the Dionadair with her.

"I don't think it's smart to sneak around like we're guilty. Then if we're caught, they'll know we're up to something. If we travel by day, on the main roads, unafraid of being stopped at any checkpoints Nathair has set up, then a handful of fake Subject IDs will do the work for us. We'll hide the stone, wrapped up tight, in the back of the truck, and have a full load of...what do they sell off up here?"

Rob pulled his flat cap off and raised a hand. "Colonial cotton. In from the ports just south."

"Okay. So..." Aini chewed the inside of her cheek. "I'm guessing we don't have access to a bunch of raw cotton, but we could simply bring clothes in for resale at the market, right?"

"I suppose," Rob said.

Thane paced a line behind Aini, his boots knocking along the wood floor. "Who all should go? Because I think we should travel in two groups with the first communicating with the second on what lies ahead."

"The first vehicle will serve as a scout?" Vera asked.

"Yes. Agreed," Aini said. "Who wants to go? I think we should have a decent-sized group to make a strong showing at Inveraray."

Thane clicked his tongue. "I see what you're saying, but remember the Campbells and the clans who support them hate the Dionadair. We don't want it to look like we're staging a coup."

"But we are."

"Aye, but let's say it's more of a changing of the guard with a Campbell still in place as chieftain."

"Yes. That makes sense. So Thane, Bran most likely, Neve, Myles, Dodie, Vera—"

"You couldn't stop me if you wanted to," Vera said.

"And that's why I added you to the list," Aini said. "We need someone who knows the area. Maybe a former kingsman or two to sway the unwilling?"

Vera pointed out two Dionadair. A woman with a long, skinny neck and thin lips and Rob. He kept looking from Vera to Thane to Aini with worried eyes.

The woman bobbed her head to Aini. "I'm Samantha."

Rob shook Aini's hand. His palm was sweating.

"You sure you're up to this, Rob?" she asked him.

"I am. But we are going to take proper weapons, right? Because you know they'll be ready to off us the second we don't seem like we are who we say we are," he said.

Thane clapped a hand on each of the rebels' shoulders. "We'll have weapons. Hidden, but ready."

"I really don't think they'll expect us to come right down the main road in bright sunlight. I think this will work," Aini said.

Please let me be right.

"Well we won't know until we try it," Dodie said gruffly.

"What are we doing about the arrival? Do we just walk up to the door and knock?" Vera asked.

"I have the password for the gate codekeeper. But I'll also speak to my mother," Thane said. "She might have an idea who would support us. I have one idea... I tried her once already. I'll do it again now." He walked under the door's white arch, phone on his ear.

"I think we should leave tomorrow afternoon," Aini said.

"That soon?" Neve said, eyes wide.

"We have to. Nathair is gone. Who knows when he'll turn around and come back. We should go now while he is out of the way."

Thane stepped back into the room. "Her phone's been disconnected."

Aini's heart gave a jolt. "Has this ever happened before?"

"No."

"Maybe it's just the service," Neve said. "Sometimes when I tour up here the towers don't have enough—"

"It's not the service." Thane pressed the phone against his forehead. "Something has happened. I have a bad feeling about this."

Aini rubbed a hand over her stomach. She had a bad feeling too, but she wasn't about to tell him and make his worry worse. "Let's get the IDs made and dress to leave. There's no reason we can't leave when you want to."

"There is one clan leader who will fight this no matter who shows up at Inveraray. My old second cousin, Sorley Menzies."

"Now *that* is a name," Myles said.

"What is it that makes him a problem specifically?" Aini asked.

"He hates everyone."

"Everyone? Come off it." Vera crossed her arms.

"He has never liked my father. Loathes me. Never approves of what anyone does really," Thane said. "He wants to be the cock that rules the roost. He caused a big fight back when I was fourteen or fifteen. Something like that. Nathair hired a group of covert experts from Cornwall and Menzies didn't like it."

"You don't know why?" Aini asked. "If we could untangle his motivations, we might figure out a way to get him on our side. Is he simply after power for power's sake? Or does he want money? Does he have a family?"

"She's kind of scaring me and I like it," Myles said.

"I suppose he wants power for power's sake," Thane said. "He has a family, although I've not seen them for ages. Not since I was a wee mite. He has two boys near my age and a wife who cares more for her own side of the family than his."

"It'd be very good if we had someone to help us go up against him," Rob said.

"Honestly, I think an ally is key. We should make some inquiries. Discreetly, of course. Bran could help with that," Thane said. "Maybe even head into Perth to see my family there."

Aini bit the inside of her cheek. "But we don't have time."

"We must make time. We need a strong ally. Especially if they've decided my mother isn't to be trusted. She'll be no help to us and we'll be no help to her without more internal support."

"We should go to Inveraray first. See what is going on and who has sworn sole fealty to Nathair, outside of the king's knowledge, and all that. Pretend to be all in. Your mother will help us sell that. We can make a plan there. Then maybe search for more support if she says it'd be a good idea."

"We can't rely on everyone else, Aini. You and me, we have to make the decisions here. Everyone is looking to us."

"And we will. But we need to scope out the situation there. They don't even know you are on the rebels' side yet. You can use that. Until Nathair knows the truth of what happened on Bass Rock, you're still a loyal Campbell and welcome at your father's estate, right?"

"I believe so. When I went back to gain their trust before Bass Rock, I went off with Rodric and only Rabbie and Seanie were there. Rodric reported back to Nathair about my...return. No one else knows what went on outside of their group, the group who went to Bass Rock."

"We only have a tiny sliver of time to use the rest of the Campbells' ignorance. I say we go for it."

"By ourselves."

"With the Dionadair that don't look like Dionadair."

Thane spun and growled quietly, rubbing his hands through his hair. "This is a mess."

Tentatively Aini smoothed her palms down the warm muscles coiled around his shoulder blades and lower back. The shape of him comforted her and made her feel like they could do anything. She only hoped he wanted the touch as much as she did. It seemed like maybe he was all right with forgetting about love when they had a war to conduct. She felt like an idiot wanting it herself. But she did. She needed the comfort, the camaraderie.

He turned, then looked at her through his fingers. Streaks of pure white shot through the gray in his eyes like there was a lightning storm inside him just waiting to be released. "I have an idea. But I don't know if it's a good one. It's risky." The room's red light painted his tattooed fingers and made them look muddy.

"Tell us," Aini said, loud enough for the rest to hear.

"I spent a lot of time at Uncle Callum's estate, learning to shoot and doing some ground fighting training. He isn't like...Nathair."

Aini could tell he'd almost said father.

"He used to talk Nathair out of his rages. I'm thinking he might be persuaded to join us. If he doesn't agree, then he'll definitely report us."

Vera shot out of her seat in a cloud of perfume. "How many men does he have?"

"I'm not sure. But more than most of the other clan leaders loyal to the Campbells. I think he's second only to my clan."

My clan. He'd claimed his clan. This was progress. Aini imagined him in Campbell tartan and tried to feel good about it. This was what they had to do. Make it so that everyone in Scotland who saw Campbell tartan began smiling instead of running off in a panic.

"Where is this benevolent uncle with the army and a good head on his shoulders?" Myles leaned forward, arms on his paint-stained trousers.

Bran walked in and took a seat beside Thane.

"In Perth," Thane said. "He lives in the old castle there. It'll take...about two hours, maybe less, to drive there. Then a couple hours travel to Inveraray."

"Ah, so we're going to visit your Uncle Callum?" Bran nodded, thinking. "That's a good idea. He'll take some persuading though."

"Aye. And I'll need to talk to you about a job after this if you're all right with that," Thane said.

Bran nodded. "Course."

The sun rose higher in the sky, and the room's light shifted from red to orange, dispelling the shadows by the clock as well as some of the bad feelings in Aini's chest and stomach.

"We can do this," she said. "Let's get started."

CHAPTER 6
HAIR DYE AND SECRETS

In the basement of the safe house, Thane followed Aini, Vera, and the rest of the group that would head toward Uncle Callum's estate. Two other Dionadair trickled in holding scissors and bottles and strips of silver foil. Aini tapped a finger nervously against her peachy, light brown cheek, and all Thane wanted in the world was to scoop her into his arms and take her away from all of this. Preferably to a room where they could be alone for a few minutes and talk. He'd love to listen as she discussed a list of tasks that had to be accomplished, fingers ticking off each item and eyes narrowing as her mind whirred. It'd be heaven to touch the velvet skin just under her chin, then to reassure her that he was behind her every step of the way on this wild journey.

So much was happening so quickly.

Aini smoothed her borrowed shirt with quick hands, then leaned toward Neve, saying something that made Neve take her arm and give it a comforting squeeze. Myles crossed his arms as he looked at Dodie; he'd never forgiven him fully for the fight in

Greyfriars kirkyard. Long-necked Samantha and that level-headed man with the cap, Rob, talked quietly, their gazes flitting from Aini to Vera before landing on Thane. Their faces were unreadable under the strange basement lighting. They gave him a respectful nod. He smiled back, hoping it didn't look too strained.

The recessed lights' pearly haze made the whole room and everyone in it look like a dream—faces blurred a bit, Thane's heart beat too quickly, and he felt as if the odd lighting would grow paler and paler until he was overcome and stopped breathing entirely. That last feeling, the sensation of being overwhelmed, reminded him of his Dreams. The prophetic ones. It was wrong to wish it, but he definitely wished he never had those Dreams. They would most likely help the rebels succeed and detach the English king's hold on his homeland, but who knew for sure? And in the meantime, they were very, very unsettling. Trying to grab hold of their meaning, to be certain it was a *Dream* and not just a *dream*, was like reaching out for a minnow in a storm-flooded river.

After a Dream, Thane experienced pain in his head as well as a feeling of being overwhelmed, taken under. The ache, now that he recognized it, told him whether his sleeping visions were prophecy or simply his brain processing stimuli from the day gone by. But what if the headache faded before he really woke up and he missed it? It wasn't easy. Not even a little. He suddenly craved the surety of a formula written in pencil on a piece of paper and the bubble of carefully measured chemicals in a test tube. Why couldn't life be more like science?

Vera raked through her large, silk bag, then held up a stack of paper—tiny slips that she handed out. There was a sketch of a person on each one, done in some kind of colored pencil. "Here are the ideas we have for how to change your looks."

In Thane's, he had jet black hair that had been shaved on the sides and was longer on top. And his alter ego was wearing eyeliner.

"Why must I always wear eyeliner when we go undercover?" He breathed out through his nose.

Aini peeked at his, her own held against her chest. Her mouth popped open, but she quickly closed it.

"Seems I'm due for a haircut." He tugged on his floppy, blond locks. "And to become some sort of rock star."

"But your hair..."

Thane came close, breathing in the scent of Aini's shampoo and forcing himself not to kiss her right then and there. "Aw, hen," he said, leaning in, "don't look like that." He brushed his lips over the soft curve of her ear. Goosebumps traveled the length of her neck, which of course made him feel very hot and bothered. He couldn't resist making her just as warm under the collar. "If you need something to hold on to during our private time, I'll still have these lugs." He tapped his ears.

Her cheeks darkened. At least she wasn't biting her cheek nervously any more.

Myles shoved his sketch at them. "I've got to take it all off."

Neve squinted at Myles's likeness. "You're bald!"

Sure enough, Myles's fake persona had an extremely short buzz cut that followed the lines of the skull.

Myles rubbed both hands over his mint green hair. "Well, if anyone can pull it off..."

Neve smacked his bum lightly. "Cheeky." She frowned at her own drawn image. "I'm going blond and it seems I'll have blue eyes. How are we going to manage that?"

"We have contact lenses ready for you," Vera said.

Aini flipped her sketch so everyone could see. It was her face but with heavy eyeliner and cropped, colored hair. "Purple?"

"Sure." Vera winked.

"What happened to the whole 'Our Seer' respect..." Aini mumbled, tucking the ID into her waistband and starting toward the long, trough sink where the two other Dionadair that had followed the group set up bottles of what had to be hair dye.

Aini sighed. "I'm going to look like an eggplant."

Thane wanted to chuckle with her, but his heart started hammering again and he suddenly wanted out of this room.

Vera snickered as she headed for dye. "You'll look great. The lot of you. In a few hours, someone will come to take our photos, then our ID man will have everything ready in minutes."

Sweat dampened Thane's back and palms. They were doing this. Changing their looks to head into the fray. There was no escape after they did. And he would have to lead them after all was said and done. If they made it through. He couldn't picture himself as a ruler. Not even a little bit. Especially with a stick of eyeliner in his hand.

"Are you okay?" Aini's big brown eyes stared up at Thane.

"Not really, but I have to be anyway, don't I?" He swallowed and tried for a smile.

"You can take a break upstairs. They can't complete all the cutting and dyeing at once."

A weight pressed against his lungs. "No. I'm not leaving. The heir can't be off for a kip while the rest go on to fight for glory."

Aini's mouth stretched into a grin. "I'm glad you're staying."

Thane forced himself to breathe slowly in and out. He wondered if this was how Aini felt when she was in tight places. What was his problem though? Just the stress of this?

Shoving his glasses into his hair, he walked over to where Myles sat in a chair. Under the snip of a young Dionadair's scissors, his hair came off in thick, green chunks. Thane allowed a slim girl to swathe him in a barber's gown and settle him into a chair. Aini stared at him from across the room where Vera shook one of the dye bottles. He realized then he'd walked away from her without saying anything. He hadn't meant to.

The girl snapped the barber's gown tight around Thane's neck. It itched. "So you'll be Chief of Clan Campbell in a matter of days and leader of all Scotland in as many weeks if we don't all die in the effort." She whistled. "That's a lot to take in, aye?"

The air suddenly left the room and Thane's eardrums pounded.

"I suppose. But one thing at a time, as our good Seer likes to say."

First, travel to Uncle Callum's in Perth without getting caught.

The wooden chair squeaked under Thane and bits of his hair slipped by his face to fall into his lap.

Thane looked at Myles from the corner of his eye. "I had no idea a rebellion would be so..."

"Hairy?" Myles supplied.

"Exactly."

Aini let Vera lean her head into the sink. Water hissed from the tap. "Thane," Aini said, "did you finish that batch of Bismian?"

Bismian was a powerful blend of bismuth and various other chemicals. He hadn't tested it properly yet, but Thane's hypothesis was if as much as a teaspoon came in contact with a victim's skin, the result would be a headache that would keep them from putting up a fight. The stuff would also erase the day's events from their memory. Bismian would be a good weapon to have on hand.

"I did. Have two vials of it in my bag and ready to go," he said.

Thane suddenly missed Bran. He was the only one who truly

understood what all this meant to Thane. He knew what Thane had gone through, had listened to all of Thane's stories about his rough childhood and how Nathair brainwashed him from the moment he came from the womb. Soon as this hair and clothing stuff was finished, he'd go find Bran and make certain he still wanted to go with them to Inveraray.

Neve came out from behind a white screen. A billowy top and pencil skirt made her look more like her fake persona. That skirt would make fighting difficult. Thane wondered if he should suggest a change.

Samantha adjusted the collar of Neve's shirt. "It fits well. Now take it back off so we can get your hair done."

Neve headed back behind the screen. "What else do we have in our unusual arsenal?"

Aini winced as Vera splattered purple dye over the top of her head. "We have the Cone5 taffy. It might help me see more spirits." She frowned. "That sounds so strange," she said to herself quietly.

Myles shivered dramatically.

"We also have a batch of gravity-reducing hard candies," Aini added, "the vision-inducing gum, aphrodisiac cherry drops—the regular formula—and we also have the strength chocolate Thane's been playing with—"

"The what now?" Myles blinked and sat up. His hair person shoved him back into the chair and lifted the razor to finish the job.

Thane cleared his throat as his own barber switched on an electric razor. "The strength chocolate drops should increase blood flow to the muscles." The razor buzzed over the back of his head and near his temples. It tickled like fiery fingers. "It should allow for a ten to twenty percent increase in—"

Neve squeaked as shards of pottery fell from her hand and clattered to the floor. "I just broke my coffee."

"Weren't you eating chocolate earlier?" Aini asked.

"Yes."

"I have a feeling that little treat wasn't just a little treat."

"Oh." Neve went pale. "I picked them up off the kitchen counter. I...I didn't think they were altered."

Thane smiled. "At least we know they work. Be careful with any small animals you may pick up."

Myles winked at Neve. "And be careful with me later tonight." He ran a palm over his almost bald pate. He looked like a brawler. It wasn't a bad look for him.

"I tested the acceleration caramels. Or whatever we're going to call them," Thane said. "They definitely work."

"I heard about your impressive sprint outside from some of the others," Samantha said. "And about Myles being sick."

"I ate them about two hours after having the gum. Thane thinks that's why I puked."

Thane nodded. "We should remember that, everyone."

Aini's nose wrinkled. "I'm sure you're right. There could be counter effects between the ingredients."

"Aye. And unexpected outcomes," Thane said as he was moved to the dyeing sinks.

"I'm not taking any of that stuff, man," Myles said. "Not unless you make me."

Neve took a pen from her hair. It cracked as she folded it like a napkin. She grinned and Aini laughed.

"That was so hot," Myles said as Neve threw the ruined pen in the bin and rubbed her hands together.

BY LATE AFTERNOON, THEY WERE DIFFERENT PEOPLE.

"We look bizarre," Aini said.

"No. We just look different," Neve said.

Thane had shorter hair now, a little longer on top than it was on the sides. With a glance in the mirror, he thought maybe he looked older. It was the dark color of his hair. Contacts in place, his gray eyes were now green as Myles's hair had once been.

The Dionadair had dyed Neve's hair a honey blond and her eyes were now a dark blue, or so Vera said. Thane couldn't tell in this light.

Aini touched her own purple hair, shrugged, and turned to pick up her bag. "I hope this works."

She did not look like an eggplant. Her elegant neck peeked beneath the back of the shorter cut and Thane's fingers longed to explore the ups and downs of the tendons beneath the skin, to kiss the spot where her neck and shoulder met.

"Wake up, sweetie." Myles bumped the back of Thane's knee with a foot and jostled him pretty good. "Time to rock and roll."

There was no more time for thinking and debating and wondering if he could handle this. When they left this safe house tomorrow and headed for Uncle Callum's, the rebellion would be beginning in earnest.

He glanced at Aini. She studied her small hands, fisted them, then took a deep breath. Were they ready? No. Did it matter? No. It was time whether they wanted it to be or not. Only the strongest of them would survive. Aini was strong enough. Thane prayed he had the same strength to find himself standing at her side when it was all over.

CHAPTER 7
A LITTLE BREAKING AND ENTERING

"If you ask me again if I'm sure I can do this, I'm going to call you *Granny* for the rest of the week," Bran said, pulling a black, woolen cap over his thick hair.

Thane frowned and Bran saw Nathair in the look, not that he'd ever say that to Thane. "I'll make you some cookies to go along with all my granny-style worrying if it means keeping you from being the next one shot in Greenock Square," Thane said.

For all that Thane's mannerisms sometimes reminded Bran of the earl, Thane had a heart of gold. Bran would gladly risk anything and everything for his closest friend.

Myles came around the corner of the safe house. "And you don't want me along?" He shivered and rubbed his recently shaved head. "Because I will totally ride along if you need me. I've learned a thing or two from this guy and that Seer of ours." Myles poked Thane in the shoulder.

Bran smiled. "No. It's best if it's just me. I can move in and out quickly. I know the layout of a standard kingsman office. I'll be back before midnight. If I'm not, maybe send Dodie and Rob out to see if I've been taken. All right?"

Thane handed Bran a small pouch. "Aini said to give you this."

Bran upended the bag to find a half-diamond pick, a small torsion wrench, a bump key, and rake snake. An impressive little set. "Our Seer knows the business of breaking and entering."

"Aye. Her father showed her how to crack locks because she has a touch of claustrophobia."

"A good man, Lewis is."

"Definitely," Thane and Myles said in unison.

"Good luck, Bran," Myles said as Bran tucked the pick set into his jacket. "I'll set some whisky out for you."

"You're moving up on my list of favorite people, colonial," Bran said.

Myles saluted him and left for the house.

"I'll share that dram with you when you return, pal." Thane tucked his hands into his pockets as the wind kicked up.

Somewhere someone was burning a fire. The smoke carried through the night and reminded Bran of playing chess with Thane, by the wood stove in a flat Bran had years back.

With a nod to Thane, Bran faded into the crisp night, hoping he'd indeed be drinking whisky when this was over and not eyeing the end of a kingsman's bullet.

A BLOOD-RED DOOR MARKED THE FRONT ENTRANCE TO THE local kingsmen's office on Union Street. Rob had dropped Bran down the way a bit. It hadn't been much a jog to get there, but Bran was already sweating. Maybe because everything was more dangerous now than it had been. At least, it felt that way.

The office was only manned by one kingsman on a weekday

night like this one. He'd most likely be at an interior desk on the first floor, watching the television. Not too much went on in this wonderfully quiet little town. Samantha had talked to Bran before he left, telling him the radios he needed to access were on the second floor. She'd worked in this very office before going over to the Dionadair side of things.

An oscillating camera mounted above the office door turned south, away from Bran's shadowy spot beside a closed down pie shop. Bran rounded the corner of the three-story building, passing a hand over a cold pillar and sliding into the black space between the office and the neighboring post office. An industrial-sized bin sat against the wall. A second-floor window leaked weak emergency light onto the rubbish stuck under its lid. He might not need Aini's lock-picking tools after all.

Pulling himself onto the manky bin, Bran eyed the corner. Every noise he made sounded like a cannon's boom. Greenock was a little too quiet for this kind of work. The window glass was thick and old. The wood frame could be opened by a brass lever —there for firefighters—but a horribly rusted lock kept the thing from turning. If he smashed the glass, it would surely alert the kingsman on the first floor. The television wasn't that loud. Bran put an ear to the window, listening. All he could hear was outside noises—the rush of the wind and a faraway lorry several streets over. He pulled out Aini's set and went to work.

The half-diamond pick worked like a charm. The lock opened with surprising ease and the window slid smoothly out of the way. This was going too well. He stepped one foot through the opening, straddling the frame and ducking his head inside.

"Eh! What's that you're doing?" a voice called from the alley.

Bran's heart scrambled up into his throat. He leaned his head back out and eyed the swaying man shouting at him. The man belched. He was drunk, big, and twice Bran's age. Bran quickly slipped back onto the bin's lid, leaving the open window behind him. He hopped onto the street.

"I was about to steal some things. So if you don't mind, I'll be back to my business."

The man's jaw dropped.

"Oh." Bran held up a finger. "It would be very helpful if you didn't shout loud enough to raise the dead again. Thanks, pal." He pulled a flask from his jacket and tossed it to the man, hoping against all odds the idiot would catch it and not create more noise by letting it crash to the ground.

Lurching forward to grab the flask, the man belched again and nearly fell.

Bran caught him and winked. "Best get home before I decide I don't want a witness to my horrible crimes, aye?"

"Aye. Course." The drunk blinked and grinned like Bran was a fairy here to grant his wish.

Before the man had even left the alley, Bran was back through the window. A chair—or something—rubbed loudly against the floor downstairs. The kingsman was moving about.

The room across the hallway housed a wall of radios, some of which were from the last century. These small towns didn't get much in the way of financial support. It was better though really because they were simple machines and easy for Bran to work, going on Samantha's instructions. He flipped the silver switch on the one labeled Southern Route and crackles exploded from the speaker. Bran turned the thing off, his pulse flying. Controlling his breath, he listened for the kingsman. Footsteps knocked along the ground floor. A stair creaked and Bran put a hand on the cool metal of the gun in his pocket.

The kingsman coughed from what sounded like the bottom of the stairs. "Haunted. I've told them already..." he mumbled.

"...won't listen to me. Sarah's right. I shouldn't take these night jobs..."

Bran had to smile. He was happy to play the ghost. With the radio's volume dial twisted down, he switched the thing back on. Pressing the button, he spoke quietly into the speaker.

"Please report on latest location of Nathair Campbell. King's update."

Samantha had said they did a regular update on important persons from time to time. Midnight would be an irregular moment for such an update unless there was an emergency, but it couldn't be helped.

The crackling turned into a high-pitched voice. "Kingsman Broch here. Respond."

The kingsman on the radio wanted Bran's name to check against his roster. Thinking of Samantha's list of who used to work in this office, he picked one name at random. Hopefully, the person still worked there. Conversation wouldn't be an issue. Kingsmen weren't permitted casual responses.

"Kingsman Alan. Respond."

The speaker whirred and snapped. Bran turned the volume up a little to make sure he wasn't missing Broch's answer. Should he repeat himself? Or wait another minute? He strained to hear the television downstairs or the shuffling of feet.

"Earl Campbell," the radio kingsman said, "was last seen two hours ago on the M6 nearing Preston and heading south.

Bran let out a huge breath. The farther Nathair was from them, the better, and it seemed he was on his way to London. But what was he going to do there? Was he on his way to meet the king to discuss what happened on the island? Would he plan a huge attack? The king was busy with the French war, but he had plenty of advisors.

"And just who are you?" a voice said suddenly from the door.

The light from the hallway illuminated the outline of the kingsman from the first floor. He had a hand on his shiny new gun and was squinting into the dark radio room.

Bran popped up, heart pounding, and kicked the chair out behind him. He lunged, then cracked the kingsman across the chin with a right cross. The man fell to the floor.

Standing over the unconscious man, several things went through Bran's brain. He had to make this look like a petty crime, committed by bored youth, instead of a break-in carried out to gain high-level intel on the king's head of security.

Bran hurried down the stairs and into the spot where most kingsmen's offices kept the petty cash. He grabbed a night stick and smashed the cash box lock. Tucking bills into his pockets, he found a permanent marker in a pen cup by a desk. On the wall in the petty cash room, he wrote an obscene phrase about someone's mother and a hippo, then topped it off with the drawing of a raised middle finger.

"That should do," he mumbled, tossing the marker to the ground.

He went back out the upstairs window, making sure to bash the glass right before making his escape off the bin. Young, bored criminals didn't pick locks. This had to look sloppy and pointless.

A dog began barking at the sound of the glass breaking and Bran wasted no time running back into the shadows that would lead him to Rob's pick up point and the safe house.

CHAPTER 8
A DREAM COME TRUE

Aini read over the coded message her father and the Dionadair had come up with to send to Lord Darnwell. "I think this word should be capitalized, if I understand the code correctly."

Father nodded, murmured something to Rob, then made the correction.

Sent directly from Father, this message asked Darnwell and his wife, Elodie, whether or not they approved of Father's efforts to begin talks with the rebels about joining the French in their fight against King John. It was very risky. If they were loyal to the king, they would report Father.

"You're sure this is worth the possible trouble? If they show this to King John, the kingsmen will be after you until you're dead." She hated saying it like that, but this was no time to dance around the truth.

"As soon as Nathair learns what happened on Bass Rock, he'll most likely tell the king. I'm already up to my neck in this, and you know it, squirrel. No use pretending otherwise. In for a penny..."

She smiled sadly at the old phrase. "True. Now, hug me because I don't know when I'll see you next."

He held her tightly and kissed her forehead. "I will always be with you in spirit, squirrel."

Tears ringed Aini's eyes. She fought to keep them from falling down her wind-chilled face. Her mouth wouldn't work, so she simply squeezed him once more, then turned toward the road where Dionadair scurried around, readying the two vehicles they'd use for the trip.

Without looking back at Father, she climbed into the truck's front cab. It was time to go. Bran had discovered that Nathair was far away, in Birmingham at least and most likely nearing London. Now was the time to go. Tilting the rear view mirror, she watched the tear-blurred shapes of Dionadair loading the back with sacks of folded shirts and trousers. The sedan in front of them held four other Dionadair, who would serve as scouts on the road, going a little ahead of the truck.

This was it. The start of the true rebellion. One truck and one car of people who believed wholly in a prophecy made way before they were born. Aini swallowed a sour taste in her mouth. She was leading a group of rebels to tear down a local tyrant and a king. A king!

But she had no choice. Nathair had left. They had to strike now and get this moving or they'd be dead where they stood in a day.

The side mirror briefly showed Bran before he disappeared behind the truck to join the bags of clothing. Thane and Vera found spots to the left and right of Aini, Thane at the wheel with white knuckles. Myles, Neve, and Dodie sat in the back. Along with Bran, Samantha and Rob rode in the truck's cargo area to keep eyes on the Coronation Stone—in its unassuming burlap sack—and the weapons and Bran's explosives, which were hidden under a false bottom near the cab.

If someone had asked Aini a year ago how rebellions were born, her answer would've included detailed strategies and seasoned soldiers. She traded a tight look with Thane, then glanced at Vera, who nodded like she somehow knew what Aini was thinking. This was what rebellions truly were. A ragtag bunch who shared a belief in something greater than them. A collection of deviants determined to shape their homeland into what it needed to be.

As the small entourage left the tidy town of Greenock, and the group's last chance at remaining hidden to their enemies, Aini realized rebellions were born of passion and desperation. An amalgam that would either get them killed or create the life of their dreams.

Driving along the River Clyde, the land grew less and less populated. Sheep dotted flat fields, and distant hills gathered up dark, sapphire clouds. Myles began to sing. Thane swore.

"She sipped sweetly soft singing, shouts stirring..."

"...not a bit of sense," Thane mumbled, "...such a glaikit, bald..."

Aini shushed him. "At least he's making us think about something other than what we're driving into. What are the odds on your uncle supporting you?"

"Burn bright blue blaze befit born bawling..."

Thane swallowed and glanced in the rear view mirror to glare at Myles with his whole heart. "I'd say less than a twenty percent chance of him agreeing with us."

Aini's shoulders weighed one hundred ton. "Okay."

Myles kept on and someone began drumming a beat through the wall of the cab.

Thane's frown faded and a grin like a memory of a smile flashed over his eyes and mouth, making Aini's stomach do a little flip. "That'll be Bran drumming," he said. Thane's contacts made his eyes green, but the gray was still there, darkening the hue.

The drumming grew more complicated, and Myles, pretty much shouting at this point, matched the song to the rhythm. Aini tapped her disgusting boots against the floorboard and tried to think positive. After a bit, Bran stopped thumping from the cargo area. Myles laughed and gave him a quick rhythm which Aini supposed was a thanks for joining in.

"That's the River Teith." Neve pointed at the waterway they were approaching. "And there?" She nodded to the right. "Castle Doune rules the bend of the river. If you visit the courtyard, you can clearly see the rich tastes of the man who had it constructed."

Aini couldn't help but grin. Neve hadn't run a tour with Caledonia—the company she worked with—since all this madness began, so the urge to detail history to an audience was probably nigh to unbearable.

Under the castle's shadow, water undulated like a blue and silver snake. White teeth of light pierced the shimmering surface like a beast fought desperately to break through. The wind kicked up, and the truck swayed along with the tops of the dark pines reaching over the road.

"Fine Scottish weather, huh?" Myles grimaced as he looked out the back passenger window.

The scout car sped up and was soon out of sight.

Thane turned the steering wheel and leaned forward to look up at the pewter sky, his Adam's apple moving above the dip in his throat. "Aye. We might get a bit of snow before the day's out."

"It's so early in the year." Neve buttoned the top of her sweater with awkward fingers, her tongue sticking out of one side of her mouth.

"Trying not to rip anything?" Aini figured it must feel odd to be suddenly stronger than you'd ever been.

"That's right. I don't think Blaine McGruffin has any holes in her sweater." Neve tossed her newly blond hair over her shoulder and pursed her lips.

"Oh Tav Laney does." Aini rolled her eyes at her own fake ID name. She lifted one of the scuffed up boots she'd been given to wear. "Good old Tav could've at least replaced the ridiculously short shoelace, don't you think?" She wiggled the frayed end of the string on her right boot at Thane.

Neve peeked over the seat at Aini's less than fabulous footwear. "Blaine is probably going to take her shopping later for better shoes."

"I should hope so. It isn't even safe walking around with one boot half unlaced."

"Not safe at all."

The window beside Vera didn't quite wind up the whole way. Air zipped through the opening and bit Aini's ears and nose. She moved closer to Thane, enjoying the heat of his body through the canvas trousers and lumpy, knit sweater he'd been assigned to wear. His false identity was heavier than him and the Dionadair had done their best to make Thane look thick around the middle. Aini knew better. She could picture the flat stomach hiding under there and she had a pretty good idea of how warm and strong it would feel under her hands. Despite the fact that she had to keep checking the mirrors to be sure death wasn't coming at them in the form of Nathair or the king, her heart tripped around in her chest at the thought of having him to herself again sometime soon.

Tiny spheres of ice began to crack against the windscreen.

"Sleet." Thane made a Scottish sound in the back of his throat.

The clouds closed in around the sloping hills and the long, winding stretch of road as the wind whipped against the truck. Soon, the green and copper growth along the roadside disappeared behind plumes of mist and the lines of ice shooting from the heavens.

Vera's phone—rigged to block any hacks—buzzed. "Aye. What? You..." Then she held the phone out and stared at it. "We lost contact. I think they ran into some trouble."

"What kind? What did they say?" Aini's stomach knotted.

"Something about the road conditions, then the call broke off."

"Will we find them if we stay on this road?" Neve's large front teeth worried her bottom lip.

"Aye." Vera tapped the phone against her palm.

The wind blew hard, ice flying across the windscreen, and their truck surged left. A wheel caught the edge of the paving and Thane swore. He jerked the wheel and righted them. "We've got to stop somewhere. I can't see a thing."

"This is what your dream showed, isn't it?" Aini remembered what he'd said in the lab about seeing ice and the headache he had after he woke up.

"Most likely." His frown said the storm was only going to get worse.

Vera put her ear to the phone again. "Are you making a pot of stew, Shelby?" she said tersely. Then she clicked the phone off. "There's another safe house coming up. About fifteen minutes off. Just past a hard left turn. Beyond the river's bend. We can stay there until this passes."

Thunder rumbled, and Aini tucked her freezing fingers under her legs. "And there'll be stew?"

Vera snorted. "That would be nice. But the question was a code."

"Right. Of course." Seemed like half of their conversations lately were code. "Why do all of your code words have to do with food?"

"Easy to visualize and remember."

Aini raised her eyebrows. "Solid point."

Thane squinted to see through the storm. "There. They're in the ditch."

The lead car sat, bum up, in the long grass beside a low, stone wall, hazards flashing and a hand waving out the passenger window.

With Bran keeping a watch on the road, everyone gathered around the wreck. The windscreen was cracked in three places. It looked like a limb from the maple above them had fallen against the hood. The driver door was smashed in badly. The Dionadair behind the wheel moaned and held his arm against his side.

Sleet bit into Aini's cheeks. "We'll get you out of there."

The others in the scout car blinked. They probably all had concussions. The man in the front passenger seat was bleeding pretty badly. Blood covered his right eye and ran over his cheek. He wiped it with the back of his hand.

Vera threw up her hands. "Well this is fine. They'll all have to stay at the safe house. We can't have scouts with brain injuries. And the car...it's done in."

Thane wrenched the passenger side door open and soon they had everyone out. Everyone's noses were red with cold and the weather only seemed to be growing worse. Aini put an arm around the man with the broken arm and helped him into the back of the truck. She and Bran propped him up with bags of cotton clothing. When the rest were tucked away, Thane started their journey again.

Vera leaned over the seat and pointed. "The safe house is just there."

Thane growled. "This hard left might put us in the loch."

The wipers squeaked and lashed along the glass, but they did little to clear the view. He swore again and made the turn. A small house with limed, white walls and a thatched roof peeked out of the sleet in a field beyond the road. It looked like it hadn't been updated since the 17th century. The icy rain paused for a minute and a barn materialized behind the house, a low, gray rock wall surrounding it.

The rain, starting up again in earnest, cut Aini's cheeks as she led the group to the door, Vera at her side. Vera knocked on the chipped paint, and a woman with very short, light hair answered holding a cup of something steaming. That little cup looked like the cure for every ailment in the universe.

"Please tell me that's tea." Aini wiped her boots thoroughly on the beaten down doormat.

"Come in then. Come in," the woman said. A silver chain ending in a copper star hung from one ear. "I'm Shelby. I don't have much, but the Dionadair are welcome to it all." She began to fuss over the injured, pulling bandages and alcohol swabs from cabinets and drawers.

Bran shut the door as everyone twisted and huddled, trying to find somewhere to stand or lie down between the round kitchen table and two sad lumps that had probably been chairs once upon a time. A fire snapped from the hearth and brightened the room.

Thane put his backside to the fire, eyes closed. "Ah. I can feel my arse again. You all right, man?" he asked the one who probably had a broken arm.

"Of course he's not okay," Aini snapped.

Shelby looked up from her work. She was wrapping a length of flat wood against the arm. "He'll be fine. It's a clean break."

"How do you know?" Neve asked gently.

"I used to be a nurse. Worked with the coast reserves until that sleekit king of ours cut my wage, raised my tax, and gave my poor sister a heart attack." She glanced at a picture hanging above the fireplace. Two blondes stood side by side, smiling and holding fishing rods heavy with a salmon each. Shelby muttered something in Scots Gaelic.

Bran found a spot next to Thane and slicked ice from his thick, brown hair. Some hit the fire and it sizzled.

Shelby seemed to know not to ask questions, but Vera gave her a minimal explanation that would keep the woman enough in the dark as not to be in danger if someone came asking questions. Shelby nodded as she brewed up two full pots of tea.

Neve took a steaming cup from Shelby and handed it to Bran. He smiled and handed it on to Vera who downed it in one go. Shelby and Neve doled out more tea around the room. The scene reminded Aini of the family gathered after a funeral. She coiled her fingers around the tea Shelby gave her and inhaled the bittersweet scent. The hot drink eased down her throat and dispelled her shivers.

As if angry they'd escaped, the storm beat against the three square windows, sleet clicking like claws against the panes. It looked like night, although it wasn't past four in the afternoon.

"I'll send up some transport for you lot," Vera said to the injured scout car group. She looked to Aini, then Thane. "We'll have to go on without them, I think, and take our chances."

Shelby sipped her tea. "You probably shouldn't have taken

this main road. There are kingsman at every crossroad. They're tailing some escaped sixth-senser, as I heard it." She jerked her chin toward a radio above her sink.

"May we turn that on?" Aini asked, heading toward the old device.

"Of course."

The knob creaked, and a voice echoed through the scratchy speaker.

"...and the forces assembled along that coastline had to fall back. The French have stated they will only hold the port until King John agrees to the first step in the peace treaty process. For now, London suffers shortages that we are certain King John will address in the near future..."

Neve snorted. "Right."

"...and the recently exposed plot to abduct the French ambassador..."

"May I suggest some rest? You lot look like you could use it." Shelby gestured to an open loft level above the kitchen where a single bed had been pushed against the wall. A woolen quilt hung from pegs and a space heater sat at the top of the narrow ladder. "It'll be tight." She eyed the group. "But it'll be cozy." She winked at Thane, who looked down fighting a grin.

They didn't have time to rest though. Nathair could find out that Thane and Bran had betrayed the group at Bass Rock at any moment. He could be sending men to find them now. Or alerting those at Inveraray, which would ruin the plan.

"We really need to stay awake," Aini said. "We'll have to get going as soon as possible."

Shelby maneuvered around Dodie to get to the kitchen sink. She filled the larger of the two tea pots again. A teal cat with a hopeful grin covered the side. Its tail ran along the handle. "I can tell you, I've lived here all my life and you'll not be leaving here until the morning."

The radio kept on.

"...weather keeping kingsmen on alert as they search for the woman accused of being a Ghost Talker. She was located originally in Skye where she told locals the spirit of a Viking raider warned of a coming political upheaval. Ridiculous and traitorous, both..."

Aini rolled her mother's ring around her knuckle, then slipped it to the next finger. Everyone stared at the radio.

"...and it spurred a group of insurgents to raid local law enforcement. Nine of the rebels were killed in front of the kingsmen's office. A man speaking for the Campbells stated that the king should see this as a sign that Scotland needs help."

"Speaking for the Campbells...I wonder who it is," Thane said quietly. "He is certainly brave, calling King John out like that."

"You all look half dead," Shelby said. "Go on and rest. You can plot to your hearts' content after you've dozed a bit."

Thane looked at Aini, a question in his eyes.

Aini sighed. "I guess we'll sleep for a little while then. If you're sure this weather isn't going to improve."

"Och, I'm sure. I'll keep an eye on the road," Shelby said.

MYLES WAS SNORING BEFORE AINI HAD EVEN FINISHED rolling out her blanket beside Thane. He covered his mouth and laughed. "Feels like home."

She snuggled up beside him, breathing in the scent of him, soaking in the warmth of his long, lean body. "Is this okay?"

His chuckle rumbled in his chest and against Aini's cheek. "Course it's okay. Why would you even ask?"

"You seemed...distant earlier today. In the basement at the other safe house." She didn't want to accuse him of keeping something from her, but that's really what she feared.

"Och. It's just a big heap of madness, this whole venture."

She leaned back. He'd removed his contacts and stored them in his bag. The nightlight Shelby had plugged into the wall near the top of the ladder and the grassy color of Thane's sweater turned his eyes the color of a summer ocean.

"So you still..."

His gaze touched her forehead, nose, and chin. She knew her skin was oily after being in such tight quarters. She should've washed it properly when she had her allotted time in the one tiny bathroom.

"Yes, Aini MacGregor. I still." His breath warmed her skin.

She was suddenly very aware of how their stomachs pressed together. His hand lay on his thigh, but his fingers twitched like they wanted to move toward her. His chest rose and fell and she was definitely breathing too quickly.

"Do you think everyone is asleep?" Aini whispered.

The nightlight flickered and someone beyond Bran, who slept beside Thane, shifted and made the loft's floor creak.

"I think so." It was odd to hear a nervous note in Thane's voice. He reached out a hand and ran a thumb along Aini's jaw.

She really and truly hoped everyone was sound asleep. Because she wasn't sure she'd be able to slow down once they started this. Thane's waistband had slipped down and his boxers showed just a little. Aini brushed a finger along the cotton edge. Thane exhaled and swallowed loudly enough for her to hear. She fanned fingers over his bare stomach. Her heartbeat drummed in places she'd never known it could. Thane covered her mouth with his and he pulled her even closer.

"Sorry," he whispered.

"Don't be." She was breathing like she'd run all the way from Greenock.

Her hand had a mind of its own. It slid down his side, feeling his goosebumps, then rose and fell over his hipbone before stopping under the edge of his boxers. The skin was so warm there. And if she went further...

Her face was on fire right along with the rest of her.

He kissed her earlobe and caught it gently between his teeth. "Aini," he breathed.

With her other hand, she pressed his lower back and urged him closer, closer, closer. She could tell he was as happy to be here as she was. He rolled, and she was under him, the longer hair on top of his head hanging down and tickling her face. Adjusting his elbow, he arched his back a fraction and his body pushed against hers. Fingers of heat rose under Aini's skin, before traveling down her torso, arms, and legs. Aini thought maybe the world had ended and she was in heaven. This was their own beautiful space filled with hope and heat, trust and wanting. The muscles of his arm tensed as she clasped his neck to draw him in for another slow, soft kiss. He broke away, his lips floating above hers.

"We should stop." His gaze went to the others. "I need to stop now."

"Please don't. I might die."

He laughed quietly and put his forehead to hers.

"You're not as crafty as you think you are," Vera said, her back turned away.

Aini's heart stopped.

"Get to sleep, you two," Vera said. "You'll have plenty of time for that when we're at your fancy uncle's place."

Thane glared Vera's way and growled something in Gaelic before rolling off Aini.

Aini had no idea what to say, so she simply curled against him, one arm across his chest, and tried to stop thinking about what could've happened. As she pushed the wanting out of her mind, her earlier worry surfaced. Thane was definitely keeping something from her. Not a terrible secret like he had before with his father and who he really was, but another type. How worried was he about claiming the role of chieftain and Heir? Would he follow through or disappear when push came to shove? He wasn't a coward. Definitely not. But that look in his eyes when he said he was fine...

He wasn't. Somehow she had to get him to open up. If he didn't, he might not be ready when they needed him most. Worse, he might destroy himself from the inside out.

"So the storm Dream. It did come true."

"Aye."

"Have you had any other Dreams?"

"I don't know."

"How could you not know?"

Turning onto his side, he slid out from under her arm and faced her. "It isn't easy to know."

"But why? You said they gave you headaches."

"I'm asleep when I'm having the Dreams obviously. I could be sleeping through some of the headaches. They're dreams. It's not like I can study them properly and come up with some way to deduce what means what and which are important."

She put a hand on his cheek. "Calm down. I'm trying to help."

Gently, he pulled her fingers away from his face and his eyes hardened. "I'll deal with it," he said. "I'll figure it out. It's my calling, right?"

He rolled to his other side. His sweater stretched against his shoulders and along the lines of his back.

Aini tugged her blanket higher. "If you need to talk about it. About anything..."

"You're here. I know. And I thank you very much for it." His head turned like he was trying to look at her without rolling back over. "I really do, Aini. But let me be on this, all right?"

Her blanket was too thin for this kind of weather. A chill spread through the thin fabric and made her shiver. Pleas and questions flew through her mind, but all she said was, "Okay," and watched the green and black spots behind her eyelids until she fell asleep.

CHAPTER 9
BLOOD AND MAYBES

A dark, deep red blanketed Thane's view of the well outside his childhood home in Inveraray. Mother faded away slowly. First her arm, then the side of her face, her white hair. Then it was all gone in the red-black blur. The sound of the birds in the pines faded to a buzzing silence. A sour odor—sweat—blocked out the scent of the resin on the tree bark and the minerals of the well water.

When Thane woke he remembered nothing of any dreams, but there was a pulsing in his right temple.

Probably just from sleeping on the wood planks of the loft.

Aini was already up, but he could still smell her on his clothing. He prayed she wasn't too angry with him. He'd snapped at her a bit last night and only because she'd been trying to help him. It was just frustrating that he didn't know exactly how to use his sixth sense.

Standing in the kitchen on the lower floor, Aini bent over a map that had been stretched across Shelby's round table. Aini's arm moved quickly as she scratched a pencil on a piece of paper. Vera, Rob, and Bran looked over her shoulder. Bran's hair was a creature born from his odd way of sleeping in one position all night.

After what almost happened with Aini, he was horribly glad his friend slept like a day old corpse. Bran would never have let him live that one down.

Aini pointed to what she'd written and took a cup of tea from Shelby. "From this map, it looks like we'll be at Hunting-tower Castle by nine fifteen, depending on traffic."

"Huntingtower?" Shelby lowered her tea cup, and her fingers covered the little yellow cats decorating the side.

Vera poked Aini in the ribs. "You weren't supposed to say that part out loud."

Aini made a guilty face as the ladder creaked and Thane joined them on the lower floor.

"Well," Shelby said, "maybe the ghost of Lady Greensleeves will tell you if your next move is doomed or not."

"Super comforting." Myles smiled with all his teeth.

"Don't let Callum hear you talk about any ghosts," Thane said. "He doesn't like anything not of this world."

"I bet he isn't a big fan of sixth-sensers then, hm?" Aini finished her tea and rinsed the cup over Shelby's demands that guests should not lift a finger.

Thane recalled the first time Uncle Callum had spoken of a sixth-senser. Some men's silence is honestly more frightening than others' shouting.

"No," he said. "He is not. I don't know why. I think it has something to do with his grandsire. The one who won their family lands back by pleasing the king."

"It would be good to know what exactly happened." Aini clicked her tongue.

Her mind was probably racing as fast as the winner of the Ayr Gold Cup. He shouldn't have compared her to a horse, he supposed, although she was lean and mean like those beauties. Good thing he hadn't said anything out loud.

Outside, the icy ground crunched under Thane's boots and the wind nipped his cheeks and tossed his newly black hair around.

Bran punched Thane softly in the liver. "Think old Uncle Callum will be pleased to see you? How long has it been?"

"Too long. He won't recognize me. Even if I didn't have this," he motioned to his face and hair, "happening. I can tell him about our talk at the clan gathering when I was thirteen though. Then he'll know it's me for sure."

"Was that the year Nathair had you jump the biggest fire and take the blood oath?"

"Aye. And Callum took me aside and told me no matter what oath I took, I had to follow my heart."

"What did you say to that piece of very non-Campbell advice?"

"I didn't say a thing. I thought he was daft."

Bran smiled sadly. "I wonder what you would've been like if Callum had raised you."

Thane touched his chest, rubbed his breastbone. "I'm not that bad, am I? Not now?" he whispered it, wishing he could take the questions back as soon as he'd voiced them.

Bran squeezed his shoulder. "Ah, lad. I'm sorry. I didn't mean it like that. You're the only one I'd follow into death. And I'm not being a prat. I'm serious. I only meant I wonder how much happier you would've been if you'd had Callum as a father instead of Nathair."

"Callum is a good father figure for the people of Perth and Kinross," Thane said. "Mother told me he built a fine orphanage for the children who'd lost parents in the factory explosion two years ago."

Bran nodded. "So he doesn't just spend money on parties and killing people like our lovely king."

"No. Callum is a good man. I truly hope we can lure him to our side."

"It's a grand idea, Thane. I think it'll work."

"It better. We won't succeed without him."

"No chance?" Thane was surprised Bran was being negative. The man was usually fairly positive in his thinking.

"I wish I felt differently." Bran frowned up at Thane's face. "I can't believe they dyed your eyebrows too. You look ridiculous."

"And I'm not even wearing the rockstar eyeliner they gave me. They can kiss my arse on that one."

"Why didn't I get a new look?" Bran plucked at his shaggy, brown mane.

"You got a fake ID, right?"

"Aye. I'm Craig Dunkirk. Aged 23." Bran wiggled his thick eyebrows and flashed his ID.

"Och, you're getting younger."

"I think Vera made this one for me. She's trying to get on my good side." He frowned.

"You're too smart to tangle with that one, Bran."

"Aye. I can't stand the woman. But someone needs to tell that to the rest of my body. In Branland, there are two warring sides."

"Time to go!" Aini waved an arm at them before disappearing into the cab.

Thane neared the truck door. "Branland. You're beginning to sound like Myles."

"You're welcome!" Myles called from the cab.

Bran barked a laugh as he started toward the back with Rob and Samantha.

THE WEATHER STEADILY IMPROVED AS THANE DROVE THE group along the main road toward Uncle Callum. Blue sky pushed out the steely clouds.

Sunlight made Aini's purple hair glow like amethyst. Her smile was radiant. "This is all going to work. I feel really good about it. You?" She touched the sleeve of his bulky sweater.

"Hey, I'm sorry about last night."

Vera rolled her eyes, then looked out the window. "Sorry it ended, you mean," she mumbled, chuckling to herself.

"Shut it, Vera," Thane and Aini said in unison.

"I meant I'm sorry I barked at you a bit. About the Dreams."

"It's okay. I imagine it's tough to get your head around being a Dreamer and the Heir."

"Ah no. It's easy. Predict the future. Rule a country. All with zero experience. Kid stuff, really." He'd tried to joke, but his tone had been tight in all the wrong places and he saw it in Aini's softened gaze.

She ran a finger over the curve of his ear, sending shivers down his back.

"You're not alone."

Her lips lifted into a half smile and he wanted more than anything to press his mouth to hers and taste her lip gloss and feel the tip of her tongue on his.

"Road, Campbell. Eyes on the road, if you please," Myles said from the back seat. "I want to die in a blaze of glory. Not the blaze of a car crash, thank you very much."

"No one is dying." In the rear view mirror, Thane watched Neve cross her arms. Then she seemed to think better of it. She grabbed Myles tight and nuzzled into his neck.

"I'll talk about dying every other minute if this is the response I get," Myles said.

"Shh," Neve said. "Don't ruin this lovely moment with your mouth."

"I hate that we have no scout," Vera said.

The road twisted and showed a truck parked and blocking three cars.

The side of the truck boasted the lions of England. Hanging from a huge hook on the back of the truck, a metal cage bore the sign *Sixth-Senser*. It was an exact copy of the cages the king always had at his parties.

Thane's stomach turned to ice.

"No." Aini's voice was a whisper.

Thane wanted so much to hide her inside his stupid, giant sweater. No side roads branched from this one. There was no escape. They would be seen. They might be questioned.

Myles's hands appeared on the seat, his knuckles white. "Turn around. Just turn around and get the heck out of here."

Thane shook his head. "It'd be too obvious."

Six kingsmen—one in Campbell tartan and the others in government black—poured out of the truck and toward the nearest car. They shouted something unintelligible at the driver.

"Who cares about obvious if we can get away? I don't want to be killed before we even have a chance to do anything." Myles's voice was raw like he'd been screaming. Purple circles hung under his eyes.

The driver of a red car lowered the window to talk to the kingsmen.

Aini clasped Thane's arm, her fingernails biting his skin. "What are they doing? I can't see." She craned her neck to look out the windscreen and see beyond the cars behind the red one.

"Well, I think we all know they aren't doing anything

awesome," Myles said. "Get us out of here, man." He pulled at Thane's sweater.

Aini gripped Myles's wrist. "Calm down. Everyone calm down. They might just ask her a few questions, maybe rough her up a little, then let her go. It's best we stay here and stay quiet. If we make a fuss, they'll take us all in, including that poor woman."

Thane was very glad to hear her managerial voice. That's what this group needed. A level head. But despite her sure tone of voice, sweat beaded on her forehead and upper lip.

The kingsmen ripped the red car's door open and pulled a woman from the driver's seat.

A man crawled from the car, reaching for the woman. "Leave her alone. She isn't a sixth-senser. I told them that already. She was already questioned. We are loyal to the king!"

The woman spat at the two kingsmen who held her. The tallest of the two cracked her across the mouth. The man with her flew at the kingsmen who easily shoved him to the road. With a shout, the woman drove a knee into the closest kingsman's groin. His associate threw her to the ground and raised his stick.

Thane saw Aini there on the road instead of the stranger.

Her terrified eyes.

Her hands raised to defend herself.

Blood streaming from her mouth.

Thane was out of the truck and running before anyone could stop him.

"Stop!" Aini was behind him, but Thane couldn't hold back now. They were beating that woman and man and it could've been Aini. His mind didn't see the error—the fact that he'd now dragged Aini right into the fray. His heart pounded and he had to DO SOMETHING.

"Hey!" Thane waved a hand. "I doubt you've put her through a proper trial, hm?"

Rage stretched his voice and sharpened his senses. The road smelled like oil. The sky was too blue, too dark, too much. The blood on the woman's face was the brightest red he'd ever seen. Aini's and Vera's boots, only a step behind his, popped along the ground like gunshot.

As a group, the kingsmen straightened. "And that's none of your business," one with a wide face said.

"It's everyone's business!" Vera stuck out her chin and looked ready to fight.

So was Thane.

Thane hit the kingsman hard in the throat. Another set of hands was on him, tugging and hitting, then Thane was punching another kingsman.

A woman screamed. Not the sixth-senser. Samantha landed in the tall grass on the side of the road, her face contorted in pain.

Rob's cap flew off as he lunged at a kingsman Myles was kicking between the legs. The kingsman shoved the kick aside expertly and spun to throw an elbow at Rob.

A fist rocked Thane's head back and light flashed behind his eyes. He stepped back dazed, then was shoved to the ground.

Beside him, the kingsman downed Myles. The colonial struggled against the man as he tried to tie him up. Myles threw out insults about the kingsman's mother that would've been funny on another day.

Vera elbowed another kingsman in the face, but he took the blow like a real fighter. The man grabbed her arm, pulled her close, and hissed something probably really vile into her ear. He tossed her against the kingsman truck and held her in place with his wooden baton.

Aini lay near Myles's feet, her eyes on fire. A Campbell kingsman started rummaging through her pockets. The Campbell colors on the man's kilt were another punch to Thane's spirit.

"Get your hands off her!" Thane rose up and was knocked across the head.

"Search them for their IDs," the kingsman above Thane said.

Where was Bran? Rob, Myles, Aini, and Neve were all captured. Samantha lay bleeding and still, near the roadside. Her trousers were bunched up and she'd lost a shoe.

The kingsman jerked Thane's back pocket open and ripped out his wallet.

"You should have to take me to dinner before you enjoy yourself like that," Thane said.

"Nice eyeliner." The kingsman snapped the fake ID against Thane's nose.

Thane threw the man a finger. It was better the kingsman think he was merely a minor thug rather than a true criminal.

The kingsman's boot pressed into Thane's lower back. "That's enough now, lad. Settle yourself."

Aini's captor eyed her ID. "This says you're from Glasgow."

Racist prat. He thought because she had light brown skin she couldn't be from here. Ignorant ape.

"Just moved there," Aini said.

Smart girl. That would cover her very non-Glaswegian accent.

"Eh, Hal!" the Campbell kingsman shouted. "Didn't we get a new list of rebels to keep an eye out for this morning?"

The boot in Thane's back pushed into his spine and sent sparks of electric pain down his legs. "Aye. Haven't read it yet." Thane twisted to see Hal turn on his phone.

The sixth-senser—the one the kingsmen had beaten—moaned. Someone was sniffing like they'd been crying.

Hal held up his phone. "Your girl there looks like number 23. Minus the purple hair."

The Campbell nudged Aini with a toe, and she thrashed, ready to snap the man's foot clean off. "You a rebel, darling?"

Anger roared inside Thane, fear cowering just behind it.

"Hmmm, she does," Hal said. "Get her up."

Thane put his hands under his shoulders and shoved his way to his knees. Hal kneed him in the side. Thane's breath went out of him in a blast, and he dropped to the road again.

"This one's very concerned about her safety." Hal put his face in Thane's. "There is something familiar about your features, pal."

People didn't usually see the resemblance between him and Nathair. But maybe this one did. Or he'd seen him at a gathering. Doubtful. It was only the top ranking clan representatives and members of the closer sect of the family that came to those. If this man did recognize Thane, could Thane use that fact? Maybe craft some story about traveling under cover? Only if Nathair didn't know yet what had happened on Bass Rock and therefore hadn't reported Thane as a traitor. If he knew and these men knew...

Hal lifted his phone and held it beside Thane's cheek, bumping his face roughly. "I think that you might just be—"

A great shout came from the greenery at the side of the road and Bran blasted into the Campbell kingsman, knocking the lout to the ground.

Vera did something too quick for Thane to catch, then somehow she had the baton. "The stone!" She locked eyes with Aini.

Freed, Aini scrambled to her feet and leaped onto another

kingsman's back. As Thane rammed his forehead into Hal's nose, he noticed Aini slide an arm around the other kingman's neck, choking him and bringing him to his knees.

Thane was so relieved he'd taught her a couple moves.

A kingsman near the downed sixth-senser from the red car pulled something from his belt. He raised it up.

"Tav! Down!" Thane shouted, using Aini's false name.

She hit the ground as the kingsman's gun fired one ear-splitting shot, then she scrambled toward the back of the truck.

Thane and Neve rushed the gunman like fools, but what other choice was there?

Thane took out the man's legs and Neve tore at his arms, but he got off one more shot.

Where was Aini? There was no sign of her behind the truck. Was she taking cover? Thane hoped she was, but it wasn't like her to hide when her friends were in trouble. No. She was up to something. He'd bet it all on that.

Grabbing the blazing hot gun barrel, Thane pushed the weapon in the kingsman's hand up, then jerked it free, popping the kingsman's finger loudly. Thane cracked the man's temple and watched him fall to Neve's feet. She dusted her hands and tried to look tough, but her whole body shook.

Bran dispatched the last of the kingsmen, Myles and Rob at his side.

All the kingsmen were down, on the ground, injured and vicious as hungry dogs.

The sixth-senser and her husband lay close and quiet on the road near two of the wooden batons that had bloodied them both. They weren't groaning or asking for help so hopefully they were fine.

Aini flew out from behind the truck with the Coronation Stone in her small hands and its burlap bag under one arm.

The kingsman eyed the stone. Only one seemed to react. His eyes widened with curiosity as he lay inert, injured enough not to move, beside the sixth-senser's tire. He didn't seem to know what the stone really was, but he knew enough to wonder. He'd talk. He'd tell the others. That couldn't be allowed to happen. If the kingsmen spread the word about seeing them and also a stone, Nathair would know what was going on and winning the rest of the clans over would become an impossible feat if it wasn't already. Nathair would prep a story, a great speech, and Thane and Aini and the rebels would lose this war before it even really started.

"Here!" Aini held out the stone and hurried toward him.

Then she noticed one of the kingsman who'd been knocked out. Drool pooled from the man's mouth and onto the roadway. She stopped, and her gaze dragged to the kingsman at Neve's feet. His broken finger stuck out at a nasty angle as he moaned and tried to get up. A nice goose egg was already rising from his head where Thane had clocked him. When Aini saw Samantha, bleeding and still beside the road, her shoulders slumped. She wrapped the stone up and went back to the truck.

Thane reached out a hand to call her back and tell her it had been a good idea to get the stone, even though she'd left it a bit late. But he let his hand fall. Would the stone have helped here? Why didn't it?

Rob kneeled by Samantha.

"How is she?" Neve asked, keeping one eye on Myles who'd put a foot on a kingsman's back to keep him down.

A smear of red colored the wrinkles between Rob's eyes. "She is alive. But I think her leg is broken and her nose too. She has a cut along her ribs. Pretty deep. We have to find someone to stitch her up."

Neve pulled a small bag from her pocket. "I'm no Shelby, but

I can do that." Before Thane could wonder at how amazingly courageous these people who hadn't grown up with violence were in this moment, Neve was threading a needle and whispering comfort into Samantha's ear.

"Eh, man," Thane said to Myles, not wanting to use his real name. The colonial met his eyes. "We can't leave these men here." They knew too much.

Aini appeared again, rubbing her eyes. Blood caked the skin around her wrist and a red slash glared above her eyebrow. "We can tie them up. Leave them behind the hedges there."

"But the truck. More kingsmen will see that truck and find the men and our story will be told."

"We have to..." Aini's tone flattened. "We have to kill them."

"You were hoping the stone would, so what's the difference?" Myles scratched his almost hairless skull. Bones gleamed under his skin. "Why didn't the curse work for this? Where were the kings this time?"

Neve looked up from her stitches. "I'm thinking our friend here must be in contact with the stone for the curse to function," she whispered, obviously meaning Thane.

Aini swallowed and held her stomach with splayed fingers. The blood on her hands was still vibrant and horrible.

"Aye," Vera said. "I think she may be right on that one. The connection between him and the stone blazed when Tav brought it out, like it wanted him to come closer."

"We won anyway," Rob said quietly, gaze on Samantha.

The weapons they'd knocked from the kingsmen's hands were black marks on the pale road.

"They are arming regular kingsmen with guns now." Thane shouldn't have been surprised. "Everything will be more dangerous now."

They were very lucky the Campbell kingsman hadn't pulled

the gun he surely had too. Must've thought he and his could handle this group. Pride in Aini and the rest swelled inside Thane, but the knowledge of what killing these now-unarmed and injured kingsmen would do to Aini crushed it flat.

"So we must kill them," Aini whispered. She tugged the gun from the Campbell kingsman's belt and held it like a venomous snake.

Thane hated himself. Despite the fact that he was rebelling, that he was the Heir, this was still his fault. It was his blood causing her this pain, his own father, his own clan.

"I'll do it." Thane took the gun, checked it for bullets, and aimed.

Bran let out a curse. "They're dead." He covered his mouth and looked down on the sixth-senser woman and her man. "Beaten to death. Gone."

Neve's head dropped and her stitching hands hovered over Samantha's bright, bloody wound.

Suddenly Thane just could not do it. He couldn't spill this blood. Not today. At least not today.

"No. We're not killing these injured in cold blood," he said. "I won't have us be like them. Help me tie them up."

Aini was nodding.

"We'll chuck them behind the shrubs and shove their truck into the loch so they won't be found as quickly."

"What loch?" Aini squinted into the distance.

"There's one not a mile from here," Neve said, staring at Samantha. "I know close to nothing about these kinds of injuries, but my guess is that she needs a doctor. Now."

Rob lifted the bleeding woman like she was nothing more than a rag doll. "I'll take her back to Shelby's. Our special friends have docs that can come there to help her," he said, meaning the

Dionadair. Thane was glad none of them knew Shelby's real name. That good woman didn't deserve trouble.

"If she worsens..." Neve bit her lip.

Bran put a hand on Neve's arm.

"She knew what she was diving into." Rob pressed his lips together as he looked at Samantha. "This is her cause and she'd be happy to suffer for it."

Rob settled her into the back seat of the sixth-senser's red car and he was gone before Thane could muster up a word.

The group gathered around the dead sixth senser and her man.

"What do we do?" Neve whispered.

They couldn't very well cart two deceased with them on this mission. But Thane couldn't leave them here on the road like this. "Help me out?" He lifted the man onto his shoulder.

Bran, Myles, and Aini worked together to gently lift the woman. They set the couple in the grass beside the road.

"We'll cover them as properly as we can." Thane began stacking stones on the bodies. The group joined in until the dead rested, protected and together.

Aini whispered a prayer and retrieved her gun from where she'd set it on the ground at her feet.

"Now!" a stranger's voice crowed.

The Campbell kingsman shoved himself up, the rest of his men with him. He grabbed for the gun in Aini's hand, but she sprinted toward the Dionadair truck. The engine groaned to life as Thane dodged a blow from Hal, then took a blow to the stomach.

Kingsmen were coming at all of them, bleeding, angry, and dangerously efficient.

Thane raised his gun and fired it into the air. Hal leaped back.

The man fighting Myles jerked, surprised at the gunshot. Myles rammed his shin into the man's groin.

Vera shrieked like a banshee, grabbed up a baton, and whipped it into another kingsman's knee.

"To the truck!" Thane snapped a palm into Hal's already broken nose, then grabbed the back of Vera's dress and pulled her toward the vehicle.

Aini drove into the fray. Everyone took hold of the open passenger door or the side mirrors, grabbing whatever they could. Neve hung off, feet swinging.

Hal held his face. "Stop them!"

A kingsman snared Neve's leg and swiped a knife at her. Blood spilled down her ankle as she broke free and clambered into the cab, past Thane and Vera.

Bran stuck his head into the window on Aini's side as Aini sped up. "We're done now, you know. They have our new descriptions. They have a good guess at least on who we are." He was looking right at Thane, his dark eyes hard.

"Nothing more we can do about it."

Aini took a curve and they fell into the cab, piling on top of one another, feet on top of feet and shoulders and hips painfully shoved together.

Gunshot smacked the back of the truck.

"We just need to drive and drive fast," Thane said. "They'll be following us until they have us or we're safe hiding with Callum. If he doesn't decide to hand us over which he probably will."

"It'll be tough for those numpties to trail us without these." Vera dug a set of keys from her bra and dangled them from a finger.

"Nice!" Aini grinned viciously, hands white-knuckled on the wheel.

But the victorious feeling died as they drove on toward Huntingtower Castle. Samantha might've died already. Rob was with her and so they were short another operative. A solid group of very angry kingsmen had seen Thane and Aini and would most likely figure out who they were and make a full report. Said report would land in Nathair's inbox along with a mention of a certain stone.

The window of Nathair being in the dark was closing fast if it wasn't already shut.

They may have escaped with their lives but that battle had been a big, bad loss, and Thane didn't see how they would wiggle their way to freedom now. Not with Nathair prepared for battle, prepared to argue against Thane's claim to chief.

He was a master brainwasher. A mighty voice one could hardly argue with. He had no sixth-sense but his ability to manipulate could definitely vie for the label. When and if they ever made it to Inveraray to talk to the clans, Nathair would have already swayed the leaders, the representatives, the cousins and kin.

Thane would end up Heir to nothing but a cruel and bloody end. Not even Aini's ghosts could protect him from a battle tipped in Nathair's favor.

CHAPTER 10
A HIDDEN ENEMY

S ilver lochs and sage green fields slid past the windows as Aini followed Thane's directions toward Huntingtower Castle. Rain that was partly ice leaked from the sky and wept onto the windscreen where it froze before the wipers could do their work.

"Why didn't I listen?" Aini tapped her fingers on the steering wheel, ticking off each thing she'd done wrong in the last twenty-four hours.

Thane covered her hand with his very large, warm one. "To what? This wasn't your fault, if that's what you're thinking."

"It is though. Partially at least."

"What?" Neve scooted forward to lean over the seat that divided the front of the cab from the back. "How in the world would anything about this be your fault? This is Nathair's fault. The king's. Not yours. Not mine. Not any of ours."

"You fought well. Especially considering you have no real training. You were amazing," Thane said quietly.

"I persuaded you all to travel during the day on main roads. I put the Coronation Stone in the back in a bag instead of in your hands where it might've done some good."

Vera shook her head and studied her broken nails. "No, no, no. We decided together, Seer. And none of us thought to have that wild candy you all make in our pockets just in case we were stopped."

Thane nodded, put a hand on Aini's leg, and rubbed circles on her thigh with his thumb. "She's right."

His newly black hair hung over one light eye. She resisted the urge to tuck it behind his ear or shift it out of his face. This road was far from straight and she needed both hands on the wheel. Especially with Thane touching her leg like that.

"You are all very nice to try to make me feel better, but this is reality. I'm not afraid to admit I made mistakes." She pressed on the gas to speed up a little as they drove past a black car that looked like it could've been an undercover kingsman. "We should've traveled less known back roads. Samantha and Rob would still be with us if it weren't for my suggestion to stay on the main routes. I should've agreed to the others' suggestion that we keep our heads down instead of throwing us into the open."

An image of Samantha lying in the dirt and grass, bleeding and broken, blinked behind Aini's eyes and speared her through the middle, making it difficult to breathe.

"Aini. Hen." Thane scooted closer and put a hand on her back. "It's all right. It's not your fault."

Stupid tears burned Aini's eyes. "Let's just get to your uncle's. We have to keep moving forward."

Vera tuned the radio to a station playing a sad song about a strange tide going out and taking a lover away. The gray tide would never bring him home again...

Swallowing, Aini focused on the winding road and began a list in her head.

We need to have altered sweets and the Bismian on hand at all times.

Unless we believe we will be searched in the near future.

We need a plan on what to do with the stone and how to protect it and use it at the same time.

The kingsman will all have guns soon.

We need more training on disarming and handling such weapons ourselves if we are to win this.

"What is our plan when we get there?" she asked Thane. "Are you just going to walk up and tell them who you are and hope things go well from there? I think maybe you should..." But her idea died before she could say it aloud. So far all her ideas had done is get Samantha seriously injured. She'd almost been at fault for getting them all killed.

"Tell us," Thane said.

"No."

He shook his head. "Fine, but you'd better snap out of this, hen. We need your brains. We should stop a few miles from the castle and arm ourselves with the altered sweets."

"And guns," Vera said.

"No, no guns. They'll see those and then it'll be over before it starts."

A crumbling car park appeared around the bend, beside a closed down convenient store.

"How about there?" Aini asked. "It's out in the open but..."

"Yes. That'll work."

Aini pulled them into the lot, and they set to work on dividing up the gravity-reducing hard candies, aphrodisiac cherry drops, vials of Bismian, speed caramels, strength chocolate drops, vision-inducing chewing gum, and golden taffy.

Bran crossed his arms. "This is too much for each of us to carry. We'll be stuffed like Christmas geese."

"I'm not having any trouble." Vera was cramming wrapped candies into her cleavage.

Neve shook her head, grinning.

"How about we each choose two to have on us?" Aini took a handful of the lavender hard candies since she'd used them several times in the past. "How high up will I go with these new ones? We haven't tested them yet, right? Neve? Did you test them at the safe house?"

"No, I didn't have time."

Aini really hoped she didn't end up on the moon. "I'll take the taffy, too. I want to give it a swing on this ghost that supposedly haunts Earl Callum's old castle. Maybe I'll see her and figure out how to better make use of the ghost kings that Thane can summon with the stone."

"That is the most kick butt statement I've ever heard in my life," Myles said.

"Just be sure you don't take the taffy and the gravity-reducing hard candies at the same time," Thane said. "Both access areas in the back of the brain—parietal and occipital, specifically—and we haven't tested the combined effects on brainwaves and heart rate and—"

Myles shushed him. "Okay, science man. She's heard enough and so have I. She won't take them at the same time, right Aini?"

"No. Definitely not." She was pretty glad Myles had cut off the warnings.

"We have enough risks going on now," Myles said as Thane nodded and walked over to inspect the candies for damage. "No need to test out the idea that science lectures can kill." Myles raised his eyebrows and let out a little whistle.

Thane whipped around, the shining aura around him glowing. "What was that last bit?"

Myles held up his hands. "Nothing, Lord Highlander. All is good. You are fabulous and science rocks."

Thane scowled, then turned back to the candy. He scooped up a vial of Bismian and some of the speed caramels. "I'm going with knocking folks out and being really fast."

"I like it." Myles grabbed the strength chocolate and some vision gum. "Can we be twinsies?" he said to Neve.

Her one crooked tooth showed in a wide smile as she snatched up some chocolate and gum too. "Definitely."

Vera had a bit of everything down her dress and Aini wasn't about to question it. She was just glad Vera was on their side.

Bran fisted some hard candies and cherry drops. "I'm good at explosions and maybe there will be a moment when we need one up high?"

Vera eyed him, almost shyly. Aini was shocked to see her look anything but brazen. "You don't need those cherry drops, love."

Bran's mouth fell open, then he broke into a laugh. "You're gorgeous, but I know better than to open myself up to one like you."

Vera huffed and stomped away.

Thane pressed his finger along the bridge of his nose, moving glasses that weren't there right now. He ran a hand over the shaved sides of his head, then through his dyed hair above. "The rest we'll store in the secret compartment in the truck along with the stone. We can't let Uncle Callum see that we have the stone until we're sure he's on our side." The glow around his hands showed up brighter against the section of hair he still had.

"Good thinking," Aini said. "We don't want to have some very visible, very wild battle that won't get us closer to beating Nathair and the king."

"I'm still impressed you can just say that sort of thing out loud without a tremble in your voice at all. I love it!" Neve patted her back. "Should we show off the stone if we win Callum over?"

"Thane, what do you think?" Aini asked.

"We'll see what the old man has to say. Play it by ear, so to speak. All right?"

"Agreed," Aini and Neve said together.

The rest gathered up their goodies and talked strategy. Myles found a boulder to sit on while he loaded candy into the secret pocket inside his thick shirt. Vera wiggled her dress higher and a candy fell onto the grass. Neve headed toward the truck.

Aini caught up with her. "Can you drive? You know this area well and I think I should sit in the back with Thane and have a talk about what he's going to say to his uncle."

"Aye. No bother." She took the keys from Aini with a sad smile. "It's not going to be an easy confrontation. No matter how it goes. This is the first time Thane will be open with who he is. With being the Heir and all. He'll really have to own it."

"Yes."

"And so will you, Seer," Vera said from behind. She pinched Aini's elbow lightly and shouted at Bran. "Will you sit with me in the back of the cab?"

"Only if you promise to keep your hands to yourself," Bran said.

Thane said something that made Bran chuckle and go a little red in the ears. "No, I won't be driving down that road, I can promise you," Bran said.

Aini eyed Thane. "Can we sit in the cargo hold and talk?"

"Sounds like you're in trouble, lad," Bran called over his shoulder.

Myles jumped off the boulder and nudged Neve, fluttering his eyelashes. "I want to be in trouble."

"This is too much," Aini said. "All these couples. I think those cherry drops leaked into the air somehow."

Thane gave Aini an appraising look. "I think we all just almost died and this is how humans respond. It's purely chemical."

"That is such a Thane thing to say."

"Is that such a bad thing?" he asked, following her into the darkness of the cargo hold.

WHEN THEY'D SETTLED ONTO SOME SACKS OF COTTON SHIRTS in the corner, knees nearly touching and backs pressed against the cold, metal walls, Aini plunged right into the topic at hand. There was no time for mincing words or being careful with feelings.

"What are you going to say to your uncle to persuade him? How do you know he won't have us shot on sight?"

"I'll tell him I want to discuss Clan Campbell and Nathair. He's brought up complaints from his townsfolk many times. It's no secret he has problems with the way Nathair helps King John oppress our own people. Rabbie told me he argued his way into a near fist fight with Rodric about the tartan law last time he was at Inveraray with the clan representatives. Said he should be able to wear any tartan he feels tied to and so should the rest of Scotland."

"So he's a passionate man?"

Thane gave her a wry grin. "When you said you'd like to spend time with me in the back of a truck, I didn't think you'd be asking me about my uncle's passion."

"Thane." She gave him a look. "I mean, passionate people make the best rebels. Look at Vera. She's a maniac."

"True."

The truck bumped them both off balance and they each put a hand to the wall.

"So we use his passionate nature to work him up," Aini said, "and persuade him to support us in convincing the rest of Scotland to do it too."

"You're a little bit scary, you know."

"I'm practical."

"Exactly."

Aini brushed her purple hair out with her nimble fingers. "How is Callum related to you?"

"Oh, his deceased wife was my mother's sister. She died a long while back."

"Why hasn't he tried to help your mother escape Nathair?"

The question scratched at an old wound inside Thane. "Because she refuses to ask for it. She is a stubborn woman, let me tell you."

Aini smiled, her teeth very white in the dim. "I'm going to like her."

"Yes, yes you are."

THE ROAD GAVE WAY TO A GRAVEL DRIVE UP TO A HULKING castle of stone. The brakes squeaked as Aini parked the truck by the gate.

Rain seeped from the grass and soaked the toes of Aini's ratty boots. Crows called from a tree desperately holding onto the last of its leaves. Trailing Thane to the pathway into the modern gatehouse—which appeared to have been added well after the construction of this old place—Aini fought a chill and shook each boot to dry it.

"Why aren't there any guards?" Myles asked, stepping out from behind Neve.

"Oh there are guards." Thane's sharp chin brushed his collar as he turned to check on Aini.

Sure enough, a man like a dragon slid out of a side door, his face ruddy and scarred. He spread his arms and smiled a smile that could definitely set someone on fire. And not in a sexy way.

"Good day, all. You do know this castle is not open for touring, aye?"

Thane's shoulders straightened. "We need to see Earl Callum."

"Do you have an appointment?"

"No. Tell him the last person to jump the fire is here."

"If I'm wasting my lord's time with a joke..."

"You're not. I swear on my mother's life."

The nasty smile faded from the man's mouth. He gave a curt bow and faced the door he'd come from. "Out here, lad," he said to someone they couldn't see. "Keep a good eye on these new arrivals."

A sallow-faced man about Thane's age walked out and glared. He had a walkie talkie clipped to his belt.

"Any news lately?" Myles asked.

Vera and Bran elbowed him hard from both sides. Aini agreed with the sentiment.

The man's eyes widened. "News?"

Myles shoved Vera away. "Has the king issued any new decrees? Are the kingsmen searching for anything in this area? What's the weather look like for tomorrow?"

Vera kicked him in the back of the leg. "Real subtle."

Sweat beaded across Aini's upper lip. "Ignore him. He's not

quite right." She gave Myles a sad smile and he sighed dramatically, throwing up his hands and heading outside. Neve stayed with him.

Thane leaned over to whisper in Aini's ear. "If they'd heard a report, we'd already be in chains."

"But they could hear about it any minute."

"Yes."

The dragon man returned and waved a hand. "Come with me."

"Myles. Neve." Aini motioned for them to catch up.

EARL CALLUM STOOD IN FRONT OF A FIREPLACE AINI COULD'VE used as a parking space. His gold-red hair shone in the flickering light, and as he turned to greet his nephew, Callum's bulbous eyes squinted. "Although I'm puzzled why you're here, lad, it is good to see you." He clapped a ham-sized hand on Thane's shoulder, jostling Thane a little which really was no small feat. "I've not seen you since you were, what, twelve? Thirteen? Christ above, you're tall."

"I've missed you too, Uncle." Thane smiled.

"What's this you've done to your hair?" He ruffled a hand over Thane's head.

"I'll explain everything. I just need you to promise you'll listen until I'm finished."

Callum's eyebrows lifted, and he motioned to a circle of leather chairs. Once everyone was settled, he leaned forward, elbows on his knees, and steepled his fingers.

"Does this have to do with Senga? You know she won't listen to me. I tried again to talk her out of that house just a year back and she hung up on me. I swear it."

"No. It's not that. But it does involve my family."

"Well, I'm ready, lad. Let's hear it. I'm not getting any younger."

Aini was relieved he hadn't shaken their hands in greeting. A family ring sparked from his left hand and having a vision right now would ruin everything.

Thane stood up even though he'd just sat down. Aini began to stand with him, but changed her mind. This was his show, and it was probably better if she stayed on the sidelines here.

Hands linked behind his back, Thane paced. "You've never liked the way Nathair runs things."

"Now, I never said those words and you know it," Callum said.

Thane held up a hand and cocked his head. Callum waved him to go on.

"It's growing worse," Thane said over the flames popping in the fireplace. "He murdered those people in Edinburgh without a trial."

"They were questioned. Some were sixth-sensers. All were rebels. They attacked Holyrood Palace, did they not?"

"There was no attack. They only hung a saltire flag on the outside. A fight started when the kingsmen showed up of course. Several were injured. None died. Their actions, while illegal, did not call for the firing squad opening up on them in a planned killing in the square."

"Why tell me? Why not talk to your father about it?"

"Come on, Uncle. You know very well how that would go."

"Do I?" His tone said he disagreed wholeheartedly with Thane, but his body language showed his true thoughts. He'd stood and gone back to the fire, his face revealing the frustration that could only come from his knowing Thane was right on all counts. Their leader was unmovable. Mad. Never swayed by the thought that what he wanted to do might not be right.

"Are you still listening?" Thane asked.

"Go on. Go on." Callum rubbed his belly like he might be sick.

"He supports the latest moves King John has made against us, against Scots, his own people. The new marriage rules? The taxes that will cripple our businesses further? You can't say you agree with his stance."

Aini wondered if he'd heard of Nathair talking to some Campbells about swearing fealty to him above the king.

"Of course not," Callum said, "but we can't fight the king."

"Especially not with Clan Campbell and its chief against us too." Thane was setting up the conversation so it'd come around to making Thane chief.

Callum spun around. "What are you saying, lad?"

"I'm saying that I found out something that changes everything within Clan Campbell and gives those like you and me— Scots who know what is right but have until now lacked the ability to speak up—the power to rise."

Callum called for his man at the door. "Take them to the guest wing. Give them each a set of clothes and take their soiled ones to the laundry. Fetch them some food. They're all exhausted from their travel and are talking nonsense." He locked eyes with Thane. "I won't hear any of that here, lad. And that's that."

Thane was losing him. The frustration and confusion that had been in his eyes, all over his face, was gone, replaced by a wall of cold eyes and thinned lips.

He had to be convinced.

Aini gripped the arms of her chair. "Aren't you even a little curious about what we found out?"

"It's a game changer, Earl," Bran whispered. His brown eyes glittered in the near dark.

Callum crossed his arms. "If Scotland were wrenched from Earl Nathair's hands, what then? You can't just go around shucking leaders off. The king would only send in another, maybe worse, replacement. An Englishman. Someone who doesn't care at all about us." He eyed Aini, then watched Thane. "This may seem honorable and worthy to you now, impressive to your lassie here, but you can't go around thinking with what's under your kilt."

Aini's fingers pinched the chair's leather arms. "How exactly could another ruler be worse?" she asked, ignoring the jab. This was bigger than her own pride. "The very man in charge of security is murdering our people with no trial. He takes innocents into his cells under Edinburgh and tortures them until they tell him what he wants to hear. How could anyone do worse?"

"Maybe let's not tempt fate with questions like that, sweetheart," Myles said, grimacing.

"Scots that don't have a job catering to the wealthiest in Scotland and England are in the worst spot imaginable. Because of the new taxes on factory workers, soon mothers and fathers won't have the money to buy food for their children. They'll starve in the street. They'll freeze to death in the winter when they lose their housing. I know Edinburgh—it is my home—and I can already see the sickness of poverty creeping up on the people there. The desperation in the kids who sell apples on the corner and the way people shrink from a kingsman who is simply walking his beat. It is the calm before the storm, Earl Callum."

The lab genius morphed into the Heir—eyes flashing, jaw clenching, and nostrils flaring. "And we intend to hold off that storm with everything we have, Uncle. Even if it means death."

Callum threw his hands up. "You're too young to know when to shut your gob, lad. I love you, but you've gone mad. To bed. The lot of you. I'll breakfast with you and you'll be gone tomorrow just after. This conversation never happened." He gave a nod, turned on his heel, and left the room.

All the air went out of Aini.

"That went well," Myles said.

Neve smacked his knee. "Shut it."

Vera swept from her chair, dress rustling. "Sleep will help our side too. He'll be in a better mood to listen and he'll have time to think on the truth you've set at his feet."

"I disagree." Bran crossed the room and faced Thane. A lock of his brown hair fell over his cheek, but he didn't bother pushing it away. "Go after him, Thane. Make him listen. He may very well report us the minute fear sneaks into him. I'll go with you, if you like, but you must go. Now."

Thane rubbed his face and growled in frustration.

Vera glared at Bran. "What do you know about it, card dealer?" Bran dropped back a step, face going slack as Vera continued. "I can tell the connection between Earl Callum and Thane is strong."

She was talking about her Threader ability. Here, her eyes alone glimpsed the colored light connection between Callum and Thane that showed their relationship. But the guard at the door couldn't find out about any of their sixth sense abilities.

"Give your uncle some space. Time to allow the shock of this to sink in. I mean, you show up on his doorstep looking like a totally different person and you're with a load of strangers...it's no surprise he'll take a bit of working to move him to our side."

For once, Vera was making good sense.

Thane blew out a breath. "All right. Fine. Sleeping will be so simple to do now that I've cracked the world open and my psycho father could be on his way here right now."

Aini touched his sleeve. He looked down, and the pain in his eyes speared her. "He won't call it in," she said.

Vera eyed the guard. "Your...relationship with your uncle is strong. Bright and true. He loves you. He won't report you. Not yet anyway."

Aini smiled. "Listen to her, Thane. We'll talk again in the morning. We still have a chance."

"Fine. Fine." Thane let her lead him by the hand behind the rest of the group and the guard. Aini hoped the man couldn't tell they'd been talking about Vera's sixth sense. That was all they needed, some vigilante ready to be the hero.

She looked to Vera, then glanced at the guard. Vera nodded and elbowed the guard.

"Where does your family hail from, pal?" Vera asked.

"What? Umm. From Inverness actually. I came here when I was ten to start schooling with the earl's fighters."

"And your family name?"

"McConoughy. We have a place up near Travars Pub."

Vera smiled like the cat who'd swallowed the bird. "And that's all we need to keep you quiet, you glaikit thing, you."

Confusion twisted the guard's features. He gave an awkward shrug and gestured forward.

The dark stairwell led to a long hallway.

"Watch your step," the guard mumbled, obviously put off by Vera. "This covered walkway's flooring is very uneven."

Warped wooden boards pressed into Aini's boots as they knocked along and came into a more open space showing more stairs and two levels of rooms.

"What happens if we see Lady Greensleeves tonight?" Vera asked the guard.

The man sniffed. "You won't. No such thing."

Vera looked at him like he was about as smart as a slug, linked an arm each with Aini and Neve, and pulled them into the nearest guest bedroom. "Sometimes I believe we'd be so much better off without the men in the world. Too bad they're the only ones who can flip my switch."

Aini threw Thane a sympathetic half-smile which he returned before the door closed. She wished she could have time alone with him, to feel the warmth of his arms and tell him it was all going to work itself out. That this was their fate and they couldn't fail. Too bad she didn't really feel that way. She was just as worried as he was.

CHAPTER 11
LADY GREENSLEEVES

With a wink, Vera sauntered away from Aini and toward the first bed in the low-ceilinged room. She flung herself down, not bothering to even take off her boots before sleep grabbed her eyelids and tugged them shut.

"Guess we should do the same." Neve took her shoes off and set them by the second bed, a narrow cot covered in a thick duvet. "You take the good one, Seer," she whispered, smiling.

Aini didn't have the focus to argue. The four poster bed squeaked a little under her weight and she tugged her clothes and shoes off, planning to sleep in her bra and underwear. The sheets smelled nice, like soap and lavender, and she hauled the heavy duvet up to her chin. Vera was already snoring. Neve waved and turned over, but Aini could tell she'd have the same trouble sleeping as Aini.

As Neve plucked at her duvet and scowled at the yellow color of her hair dye, Aini's mind churned like the taffy puller, stretching out tonight's conversation and combining it with the one she had with Thane in the back of the truck. Why would Callum be any different in the morning? He'd just say no to helping them again. He wouldn't listen. How could they stir his passion?

Eight large paintings covered the guest room's whitewashed stone walls. One was of a double bridge keeping company with a plethora of ferns, sunlit saplings, and thick moss. Another showed an old manor house with too many chimneys and lighter stone marking the edges of each corner. Several boasted a crowd of smiling people, all lined up for the photo. Children grinned and showed missing teeth. Women in fine, striped silk dresses or plain work trousers turned to look thinner or hugged friends to pose. Men sucked in stomachs and smiled over bow ties or work shirts.

This was what Callum loved. His town. His people. Somehow Thane had to relate this problem directly to them. It already was, really, but how could they argue the cause to tie it more immediately to Callum's beloved home?

Somewhere a clock chimed out the time. She'd been in bed for over an hour. Sleep wasn't happening. She swung out of bed and grabbed a guest robe hanging from a wooden post in the wall. There weren't any slippers and she had zero desire to put those ratty boots back on anytime soon, so she slipped out of the room on chilly, bare feet.

"Tav?" Vera hissed Aini's fake ID name from her bed, but Aini just closed the door, pretending she hadn't heard. She needed to walk alone to think.

Moonlight flowed over the outer room and along the stairs leading up to Thane, Bran, and Myles's room. Surprisingly, Myles snores were absent. Normally, his snoring would be shaking the floor.

"Hey," a quiet voice said, making Aini jump. Myles sat cross-legged at the far end of the covered walkway that spanned the space between the two parts of Huntingtower Castle. He waved, something small and light-colored in his hand. "Sorry. Didn't mean to scare you."

She wasn't going to get any thinking done with him around, but she didn't want to be rude so she crossed the cold floor. The wooden boards moaned and sent a shiver up her back.

Myles held his sketchbook. A chalked cow with dragon wings was paused in mid-flight on the page. "What do you think?" He held it up proudly.

"Is it a metaphor explaining the way I felt trying to talk Earl Callum into going up against Nathair?"

Myles chuckled. "Yeah no, but I like it. Really, you did well. I don't think he's coming around anytime soon though. Seems pretty ticked off about the whole thing."

"We are asking him to commit treason. That's not something you agree to right away."

The moon illuminated Myles's skin. He still looked tanned from his life in the southern colonies, but maybe his skin was just that shade.

"Did you send a message to your mother? Thane mentioned it."

"Yeah. Some of the old guys at the safe house helped me with a code based on their occasional communication with the rebels over there."

Aini wasn't about to ask if he hoped his mother would write back. She already knew he'd deny that hope even though it would be obvious in his eyes. "Do you think you'll ever go back?"

He blinked, chalk frozen above his paper.

"I'm sorry," she said hurriedly. "Forget I asked."

Wishing she was more sensitive, she pinched the bridge of

her nose and contemplated how many mistakes she'd made just today.

"I'll go back. Someday. I miss the people. They're a lot like the Scots, but more...changeable. Individually. Don't you think?"

"I've changed a lot, that's for sure. I never would've rebelled five years ago. Rules were my lighthouse beam."

"Oh, you still love the heck out of some rules, lady."

"But I break the ones I don't like."

Myles opened his mouth to reply, but a scratching sound came from the roof. It sounded like the slate tiles were moving around.

"A raccoon?"

"I doubt it."

"Because there aren't raccoons in Scotland or because you think it's something else."

"Both."

Myles scrambled to his feet and dropped his chalk. "Let's get out of here."

A light voice sang a line. The words were tangled, unintelligible. Goosebumps rose along Aini's arms.

Myles swore. "Yeah, raccoons don't sing," he whispered. His chalk sat beside his foot, forgotten.

The strange noise moved to the spot right above Aini's head and the moonlight from the window lit the painted vines and circles on the ceiling.

"I am thine, my love, and I will come to you," a deep, sweet voice said.

Myles swore some more. Loudly.

Vera popped out of the door, and Aini about leaped out of her skin. "What's that racket?" Vera demanded.

Aini shushed Vera and pointed up. "Lady Greensleeves?"

"It's not." Earl Callum emerged from the shadow behind

Myles. "There is no ghost here. And you should all get back to bed."

"I have zero problems with that directive. As you say, sir." Myles saluted and ran off past Vera and toward his room.

Aini picked up his piece of chalk and faced Callum. "And who do you suppose is singing on your roof? One of your guards?"

"He has a right lovely voice." Vera smirked.

"I didn't hear anything. Now go on. The both of you."

The scent of sage filled the air and the wall beside Aini shimmered like disturbed water.

"I don't think..." Vera started, hand going to her lips.

A woman's head, cloaked in white-blue light, moved through the walkway's wooden wall.

Aini was face-to-face with what had to be Lady Greensleeves.

Her body followed her head and Aini stepped back to give the ghost room. An emerald veil covered most of her hair and a darker green dress wrapped her small body tightly. The world shivered around her, white and blue. Her skin was a pearly gray. Her eyes were like banked coals in a hearth, burning, ashy, black, and red. The scent of sage and smoke was nearly overpowering.

"You will not stop me," the ghost said quite clearly and Aini wondered if she'd ever get used to being a Ghost Talker.

"What's she saying?" Vera asked.

Callum stood frozen, his face contorted in a mix of shock and outrage. Why was he so angry?

Aini told them the ghost's words.

Lady Greensleeves lifted an arm slowly, her dress and veil billowing around her like she was underwater. "He is to blame for my unhappiness. Before there were others, but now, now it is him." She extended one finger and aimed it at Callum.

The air was so, so cold.

"Why is she blaming you for her unhappiness?" Aini asked Callum.

Callum kept staring at the lady. "She lies. I've never seen her before tonight and I have no idea who she is, outside of the old stories. Those things happened well before my time or even my great, great grandsire's."

"Oh no. That's a lie." Vera came closer, keeping an eye on the ghost, but angling her body toward Callum. "I'm a Threader, dear Earl, and I can very clearly see a bright green and purple line reaching between you and this lady. You know her and you know her well. What did you do to her?"

"Nothing! And you—you're both sixth-sensers! You shouldn't be here. You..." Callum swallowed and schooled his tone. "I've done nothing wrong. No matter what you abominations claim this spirit says about me."

Aini clenched a fist, ready to show this earl what she thought of his opinions.

"It was my resting place," Lady Greensleeves cooed. "It was where I waited for my lover."

Aini fought the instinctual urge to run. Facing an angry ghost was less than comfortable. "Did you disturb her grave?"

Callum scowled, and his hands shook at his sides. "No."

"Come on, Earl Callum. Whatever you did, just come clean and we'll figure it out. You are a good man. Thane told us about how much you care for this area, for your home. He said you recently added a new wing to the orphanage you started when you were first given your title. I'm sure you didn't mean to hurt this lady. Be honest and we'll figure it out."

"The orphanage..." The lady began singing quietly, almost too low to hear.

"What is it that bothers you about it?" Aini asked her.

Vera and Callum stared.

The ghost covered her face in her nearly transparent hands. Bones moved under the opal skin. "He killed her right on my grave. He desecrated my resting place. He ruined it. The blood, it pains me. Pains me!"

Aini knew neither Vera nor Callum could understand what the ghost said. Only her mind could unravel the language and the spirit's noises and somehow turn them into words that made sense.

"Earl Callum," Aini said, "was there an accident near the orphanage, near the kirkyard there?"

"How do you know there is a kirkyard just there?"

"Answer my question."

"I don't know what she is telling you, but I—"

"Enough of this." Vera pulled out a knife. Where had she found that? "Tell us what you did, you evil man, you traitor to your people, tell us or I'll finish you right here."

"Try to gut me, girl, and see what happens," Callum snapped.

Aini had no doubt Callum would win this fight. She could see it in his confidence. There was nothing faked about that.

"Maybe don't wave knives at people we're trying to persuade to support us, okay?" Aini held out a hand and lowered Vera's weapon.

Vera's lip curled, but she let Aini take the knife.

Lady Greensleeves' hands fell away from her face. She glared at Callum. "She would not have spoken against you, coward. You should have given her aid."

The area around Callum's mouth had gone white and he looked ready to fall over. "What is she saying?"

"That you killed a girl on the lady's grave and you didn't need to. That the girl you killed wouldn't have gone up against you about whatever you did."

Callum fisted his hands and pressed them to his forehead,

blowing out a loud breath. "There was a car accident. I ran off the road after going to the pub. I hit a girl in one of those tiny cars, and when I checked on her, it was...it was clear she'd broken both legs to the point...to the point that she'd not walk again. She was our pastor's daughter. I'd paralyzed our greatest holy man's only child. I would've been hated. I hated myself. Still do."

Vera crossed her arms. "So you offed her so she couldn't talk."

Callum's head fell forward. "No. She isn't dead. She lost a load of blood and doesn't remember seeing me. I drove off, and no one ever found out I was the one who'd driven her into the ditch beside Lady Greensleeves' grave. No one knows. They think it was a stranger. A tourist, maybe. That it couldn't possibly have been one of us."

"She could've died on the side of the road because of your fear," Aini said, shock pealing through her.

"That's why you built an orphanage." Vera rolled her eyes. "Guilt."

"Aye." Callum wiped his face with his hands. He knelt. "Lady Greensleeves, I am sorry for what I did and how it hurt you. I will do whatever you wish to put you at rest again."

Lady Greensleeves turned to Aini. "Speak to him about honor. Clean the stain. Help me rest."

"I'd say a huge house for children who need it was a good start," Aini said. "What else would you like him to do?"

"He should conceive a plan and I will be satisfied."

"He needs to come up with it himself?"

But the lady didn't answer. Her form dissolved into nothing more than a sparkling kind of floating dust as she eased backward, into the wall. With one more line of singing about her lost lover, all noise and the sage scent faded.

Callum looked up at Aini. It seemed like he wasn't the same man they'd met earlier, the one with a straight back and the walk of a soldier. This one was humbled with red-rimmed eyes and a cross to bear.

Words crawled out of his throat, raspy and thick. "What can I do?"

"She said you had to think of some way to show her honor and clean the stain from her burial place. I have no idea what that could be." A cold lump formed in Aini's stomach. Somehow she knew she was supposed to use her other sixth sense, her Seer ability. The surety of it pressed against her heart. "Give me your hand, please. The one with the ring."

His eyes widened, but he slowly extended his left fingers. Before she could let that old fear rise up and overtake this intuition to use her gift, she gripped his ring finger.

The walkway's damp wood scent, the shadows around Callum's kneeling form, and the warped floor fell away.

A vision rushed over her head.

A rust-haired boy ran down a path guarded by twisted pines and ferns. To the boat, he called out, coming into a clearing. A group of boys and girls with dirt smeared on their cheeks and sticks in their hands turned. A crumpled form lay on the ground. The rust-haired boy drew up, panting. Purplish blue and sick yellow swirled around his head, fear and the sense of betrayal mixing equally. "What have you done to Lolla?"

"She can't say the oath right. The oath to the Campbells. She's a disgrace."

"But she's a Gowrie." *She was his sister.*

He pushed through the bigger children and threw himself on top of her. "Don't you ever strike Lolla again, you beasties. I don't care what she can or can't say!"

The children lifted their sticks and each took a whack at young

Callum before heading back into the big, gray house in the distance. Tears blurred the sight of the house's sun-hued flowers.

The inside of Huntingtower Castle and the face of its repentant master blinked back into being.

"What did you witness, Seer?" Vera said, her voice awed.

Callum's mouth opened and shut.

Aini helped him to his feet. "I saw you sacrifice yourself for Lolla, for your sister, when the children were beating her."

Jaw clenched, Callum breathed loudly through his nose. "So you have two sixth senses?" He shook his head. "Lolla died the next day. Accident, they claimed. But it wasn't. They pushed my good sister out of the tree she liked to climb and she broke her neck. I never told anyone what I suspected though. I kept it from my father and mother. They thought she was mad." He whispered a prayer and kissed his ring. "But what does that have to do with the lady?"

"Maybe you need to sacrifice more than money and time to clean the stain of what you've done. You need to tell the truth about Lolla and also about the car accident."

"My people here will hate me for my part in the accident. As for Lolla, there's not many left who even knew her."

"You'll never know if it matters until you do it," Aini said.

Without a word, Callum left them.

Aini had no idea whether she'd helped or hurt their situation.

CHAPTER 12
IN THE KINGDOM OF ALBA

Thane and Bran slipped out a side entrance to the upstairs guest room right after Myles pulled his own escape. Thane had to leave the stuffy, old place, breathe some fresh air, and try to muster up some hope for tomorrow's discussion with Uncle Callum.

"Where are we going exactly?" Bran jumped down into the trimmed grass of the castle garden from the new wall, trailing Thane like a shadow in the moonlight.

"I thought we'd go to Scone."

"Want to check out your predecessors' old stomping grounds?"

"Something like that."

Thane opened the driver's side of a sad little auto and set to work hot-wiring it.

"Ah." Bran stretched back in the seat and pretended to be relaxed when he was really keeping an eye on the road. Careful Bran. Good man. "This is just like our days before you went to uni."

"Never thought I'd miss the days of petty crime."

"Stealing cars isn't actually that petty."

"Compared to rebelling against one's father who works for one's king?"

"Point taken."

The engine rumbled to life. The road curved between a sloping hill and the rough growth no one wanted to mow.

Last time Thane had been to visit Uncle Callum, his mother had been with him. It'd been Christmas and snow had blanketed the ground. Now, the town was slicked with dark ice instead of nice, clean powder. He'd been thirteen when he was here with his mother and all he'd wanted to do was tie Callum's old hound up to a sled he found in an outbuilding and go for a ride. Mother had rescued the dog from what would've probably amounted to accidental torture and given Thane a job to do.

A science-enthusiast and baker herself, his mother had asked him to learn the secret ingredient in Uncle Callum's famous venison stew.

He remembered the moment like it was yesterday. After two solid years of doing terrible duties for Nathair, the idea of simply finding out an ingredient had been amazing. This wasn't knocking a nobleman's son into the drink to distract him while Nathair's men searched his car. No one had to be beaten down or scared to their bones with a dead rabbit in their post box. This was a clean job, a mission he could feel good about and not have to vomit over when he was through.

He'd hurried to the kitchen faster than Callum's hound could track a deer and set to bugging the cooks about cinnamon and types of Mediterranean salt.

Maybe that was why Lewis's lab had felt so right. It had been a good job. A nice thing to do. Well, aside from the spying.

Thane sighed and drove under a crumbling stone arch. Scone

Palace rose up, pointed and arrogant and lovely, lit by tacky floodlights that weren't good enough for it. Pulling into the car park, Thane couldn't help but hear Neve's voice in his ear, telling him about Robert the Bruce being crowned here. She'd know the exact year and how the clothes would've looked on that day.

Thane and Bran climbed the gentle slope to the moot hill where it was said the long-ago crownings had taken place. All Thane knew was that the wind through the towering pines and the cool air on his face was like a welcome. He felt as if he'd come home.

Bran, however, watched the wood like something was about to pop out and grab him. "I don't have a weapon. Just so you know."

"No need for one tonight."

"That is the best news I've heard in weeks."

Thane smiled at his friend and tried to hide the stirring in his wame. He wanted to appear composed and casual to Bran, not like some fainting idiot all pleased with himself, so he pushed the conversation far, far away from here. "So you really do hate Vera? She likes you, you know. And she's not hard on the eyes."

"She has a beautiful backside and a laugh I could fall into, but the woman is a snake and I won't invite a snake into my bed, I can tell you that."

"She is on our side."

"She is on the side of the rebellion. Vera would slit our throats in a heartbeat if she thought it would speed the revolution."

"I thought I was the only one who saw that. I've been trying to persuade myself to trust these Dionadair. It's no easy task." Thane took a circuitous route to the red stone chapel that backed up to the wood. The chapel wasn't what called to him, but he wasn't ready to stand where his predecessors had taken on the mantle of kings.

Bran peered into one of the chapel's windows. "You're right to watch them. Although I do think it would set their plans back a good step if they offed their Heir."

"Aye, I suppose I'm safe as long as they still think I fill that role."

Bran poked Thane's arm. "You don't think you are? After all that's happened?"

Thane shrugged. "The stone roared. The kings defended me. But am I truly meant to rule? I don't know a thing about politics."

"Och. There are plenty around you who can handle that bit for you. You're meant to inspire the people and carry out the plans you think are best for them. You can do that. I know you can. You're a good one, young Thane."

"I wish you would stop with the *young*," Thane smiled to take the bite out of his tone.

"Can't let you grow too big-headed." Bran punched him lightly in the pressure point on the outside of the thigh.

Thane stumbled a little, swiping back at Bran's mop of hair.

Snow drifted from the black sky like the stars had come down to light the hill. The air nipped at Thane's cheeks like small, rough kisses. With every step through the low grass, he wondered if *Cineád mac Ailpin*—the supposed first king of the Scots, Kenneth MacAlpin—had pressed down this same piece of earth. What had gone through that great man's head when they decided to crown him? He'd had advisors certainly. He'd been raised to rule. Thane had not. Well, Thane had been groomed at first to take the role of chieftain. But that had changed when Thane showed signs of weakness, as Nathair called it.

Thane had shown mercy to wrongdoers and to those not in

thick with the clan. Nathair had quickly decided Thane would not lead Clan Campbell, though Nathair never had settled on who actually would take over for him. Thane hadn't thought much about it. His mind had tried hard to think on it, to wonder what might happen if his father couldn't lead anymore. But he'd always pushed those wonderings away. Hopelessness had a way of making him pack his feelings and questions into certain boxes, some of which he never opened.

The wind blew again, pine-scented and soft. Thane stepped onto the flat red stones that surrounded the fake Coronation Stone.

Without any preamble, his veins lit up like he had gunpowder for blood.

He exhaled in a gust of white plumes.

Bran's eyes were wide. "My God, lad. That's..." Bran was looking Thane up and down. "I can see this *light* around you."

"Aini said she can see that light all the time since the stone roared for me."

Bran rubbed his forehead and whispered under his breath. "Amazing."

Thane closed his eyes and let the wind wrap him up, allowed the feel of the place—a heavy, sweet embrace—soak into his shoulders and along his limbs. There was a rhythm hiding in the wind's noise through the trees. Aini would've understood it, he was sure. A coolness filled his left hand, a roughness along his fingers.

"Open your eyes, lad."

Thane did as Bran said and looked down to see a pale, flickering broad sword in his hand. He flipped it upside down and set the tip on the flat stones, taking the hilt in both hands. Closing his eyes again, he whispered to the spirits of the rulers of ancient Alba, of his home, his people.

"Please help me be the leader they need. Help me find my way. Give me the formula for bringing their enemies low and healing their hearts."

When Thane opened his eyes, Bran was grinning. "Only you would ask the spirits for a formula."

Joy suffused Thane's chest and came out in a loud laugh. "I can only be who I am, pal. No more. No less."

The sword dissolved in a shower of illuminated particles and Thane was comforted with the knowledge that somehow he'd done the right thing in coming here and paying tribute, in asking for aid. Now if he could just translate this experience into practical capabilities as the Heir.

"Let's go on back, aye?" He stepped away from the crowning spot and clapped Bran on the shoulder. "I need some sleep before I battle with Uncle Callum."

The stars shimmered in the black sky. Bran stared up at them. "This is some wild adventure you've dragged me into. I never could've guessed this forgotten boy would live to serve a true born king."

He may never have known his family, but he was definitely not forgotten. Not to Thane. "I'm just glad you know how to serve a good whisky," Thane said.

With a wry grin, Bran tripped Thane, and they traded a few easy punches before heading back to the castle for some hard-earned rest.

SLEEP DID NOTHING TO CLEAR OUT THANE'S MIND AND GIVE him a rest. Sleep brought a new Dream and there was no doubt this time that it was a dark tale of a very possible future.

In the Dream, Thane stood on a mountain top that was really nothing but an impossibly huge pile of round rocks. His foot slipped. The drop to the valley below yawned wide open like a great beast ready to swallow him up. Heart in his ears, Thane steadied himself and grabbed the exposed root of a gnarled pine. He turned to see Aini. A blood-red dress whipped around her as she stood like a statue, not breathing, not blinking.

"Choose," she said.

Her dress, face, arms—all melted down and reformed into Nathair scowling, scar puckering the skin at his neck. He held up Thane's Campbell necklace and shouted.

"Choose!"

Then Nathair melted away too, leaving nothing but a stain of red-black blood on the mountain top's stones. Thane fell backward. The wind rushing past his ears as he plummeted sounded like a man's voice, Kenneth MacAlpin's voice.

"Tagh. Chì sinn dè an seòrsa rìgh a bhios thu." *Choose. We will see what kind of king you'll be.*

Before Thane hit the earth, he raised his hands and saw he held the ghostly sword from the moot hill. It was covered in blood.

CHAPTER 13
DECISIONS AND FIREWORKS

Uncle Callum's chair was empty when Thane and the rest followed a guard into a large feast hall. A mound of bright, scrambled eggs and bowls of steaming porridge crowded the table. The guard, who obviously wasn't just a guard but a butler of sorts, too, gestured to the high-backed chairs. When Thane visited as a child, he used to pretend the chairs were ships, the spindly backs like masts.

Thane sat beside Aini and to the right of Uncle Callum's place. "When will my uncle be down?" Thane asked the butler-guard.

"I don't know, my lord. I think he had a difficult time sleeping last night. May I suggest you eat? The earl won't mind at all."

Myles looked a little green around the mouth. "I wish I had an appetite."

Neve frowned. "I feel like there's something everyone knows but me." She spooned some porridge into her mouth.

Aini elbowed Thane. "I need to talk to you."

"And I you, hen, but maybe it can wait until we've talked to Uncle Callum."

"You need to know what happened last night," she said.

"I went to Scone." He wouldn't tell her about the Dream just yet. He'd wrestle with that one on his own. But he could tell her about his experience on the moot hill.

"You what?" Neve's spoon hung still in front of her chin.

"Bran and I," he said, "we drove to the moot hill where the Coronation Stone used to rest. Where the old kings were crowned."

Aini gave him the MacGregor eyebrow lift. "I want to hear all about that, but that's not what I'm talking about. Last night, Myles and Vera and I—"

"How come no one thought to invite me on one of these little nighttime outings?" Neve said. "You know what? Scratch that. I'm glad I, for one, had a good sleep." She shrugged and finished her porridge, moving on to the eggs.

Myles gave her a weak grin. "You're the smart one, Neve. You are lucky you didn't have a run-in like we did. Now, can you see any blueberries or strawberries around for the porridge?"

"You should eat it with salt and butter only at Uncle Callum's table," Thane said.

The man himself walked in. "He is right. That's the only proper way to eat porridge." The memory of a smile graced his weathered face. "I think we all have some stories to tell, aye? I'll start."

Then Uncle Callum's voice took on that rise and fall cadence he used during clan gatherings by the bonfires. He told them about Lady Greensleeves and a terrible accident. He'd called the city council that morning and told them he was responsible for the car wreck and that'd he gone to the lady's grave at sunrise to leave a blood sacrifice.

"What did you leave?" Neve asked.

"The spirit smelled of sage so I tied up some dried lengths of the herb from my kitchens and dragged my cut palm over them to bless them."

"Perfect." Aini smiled and folded her napkin on her lap.

"So...you're no longer against all sixth-sensers?" Thane asked. Uncle Callum had always railed against them, although he'd protected Perth from the worst waves of questioning Nathair set into motion.

"No, lad. I'm not. It was my own fear that drove that anger. I'm ashamed of it. Truly."

"It takes a real man to admit when he's being an arse," Bran said, giving Uncle Callum a nod.

Thane took a sip of black coffee and cleared his throat. He had to tell him. "You know the old stories about the Coronation Stone?"

"Aye," Callum said, "of course." He steepled his fingers and watched Thane carefully. The white bandage around his hand was like a flag of truce he'd raised to sixth-sensers and Thane had to make the most of his uncle's open state of mind.

"Aini here, Aini MacGregor, daughter of a chemist who once worked for the Dionadair, is the Seer. The Seer. She found the Bethune brooch and followed the trail that led to the Coronation Stone's resting place on Bass Rock Island."

Callum's face was unreadable.

"And when we touched the stone, it...well..."

"It growled like a beast and took down all those idiots working for Earl Nathair!" Myles, halfway out of his seat, raised a fist.

Callum stood and walked to the door.

"I know it's difficult to believe," Thane said.

Taking a deep breath, Callum returned to his seat. "You're saying that the Coronation Stone protected you, young Thane."

"Aye."

"And so you claim you are the Heir to Scotland's throne."

Aini raised her chin. "He is the one that will knock the king from his seat."

"You're his Seer. He is your Heir."

Neve clasped her hands and grinned. "Merlin and Arthur is my favorite way to think on it."

Callum swallowed and grabbed his glass of water, drank it down. He wiped his mouth, gaze roving the faces gathered around the table. Thane couldn't stop clearing his throat and the room felt too small even though it was honestly too big. His fingertips tingled like he was about to be attacked.

Beside Callum's hand, a phone reflected the morning sun and sent a ray of painful light into Thane's eyes. With one call, it would all be over. They'd be taken into custody and thrown in prison if they were lucky. If not, they'd be shot the moment Nathair's crew showed up in answer to Callum's report.

Thane's hand searched for Aini's under the table. She found his and gripped him tightly in her soft but strong fingers.

Callum pushed away from the table again and turned his back on them, arms crossed. "What do you suppose I do about this?"

"Support Thane, of course," Aini snapped.

Callum whirled around, and Thane wished a little that Aini hadn't jumped to that so quickly.

"In what way?" Callum demanded. "With guns? Fighters? How do you plan to overtake the entirety of Clan Campbell's forces *and* the king's, which will back them? What do you know about fighting against the king's Head of Security?"

Thane wondered...should they tell him? In for a penny...

"Uncle Callum, meet Vera Bethune, daughter of the most influential leader of the Dionadair rebels."

Vera stood up and curtseyed. "Good to meet you, Earl Callum."

Callum's mouth dropped open. "God above. You've already gone in with the rebels, then?" He glared at Thane. "And brought them to my house. Without any thought to my safety."

"Aye, but I did worry about your safety and ours and that's why I have black hair and contacts and we all have fake Subject Identification Cards. We're committed to this, Uncle. We can't back out now. Will you support us or throw us to the wolves?"

"If I do throw you to these metaphorical wolves, will a non-metaphorical, actual curse take my life?"

Thane didn't want to say. He wasn't sure how the stone's curse really worked and he wanted his uncle to do this because he believed in it, not out of fear.

"Probably!" Myles grinned and scooped another heap of eggs onto his plate.

"I need time to think," Callum said.

"Aye. Of course. But will you give me your phone as a sign that you're actually just thinking?"

"You know I have access to any number of communication paths."

"I do. It's merely a symbol of your action. A promise, of sorts."

Uncle Callum slid his phone to Thane, who pocketed it before the man changed his mind. "Thank you, Uncle. I hope you'll come to me with any questions you might have."

With yet another heavy breath, he nodded and left the room. Poor old man. They'd probably end up giving him a heart attack.

"How long do we give him?" Aini arranged her used fork and spoon on her plate, then finished the last of her coffee.

"I'll find him in an hour. If he doesn't know by then, we need to find a way out of here."

Vera brushed a little egg off her dress. "Agreed. In the meantime, we should practice with those candies of yours." She wiggled her eyebrows at Aini.

Aini grinned. "It's time for dessert, friends."

Thane looked out a window to see Callum walking the garden, hands in pockets and shoulders hunched. He didn't envy his uncle's decision. No matter what he decided, his life was never going to be the same. It wasn't so long ago that Thane had gone through that same decision.

Aini came up beside Thane and steered him out of the dining area and into the hallway. "You never told us what you and Bran did last night."

Thane broke into his tale about Scone and the sword. "I'm not sure what good it did, but..."

"I can see what good it did," Aini said. "Your aura is brighter than ever. Do you truly feel like the Heir now?"

"I don't think I'll ever be comfortable with the position."

"Me either. With being the Seer, that is. Leading the rebels. I've done everything wrong so far."

"You have not."

She waved his arguing off. "I want to talk about you."

"Well, I do feel different today. After going to Scone. Is it mad to say I can feel the blood of those kings inside my own veins?"

"Of course not. You do have their blood in you."

"But I *feel* it. It's as if I've fireworks setting off under my skin sometimes."

Aini reached up and put her arms around his neck. She smelled lovely and her skin was so warm and smooth. Her lips parted to say something, but she stopped. The corners of her mouth tipped down.

"What is it?" Thane made circles on her cheek with his thumb.

"I want to enjoy you, enjoy us. To say that I'd like to give you some more fireworks, if you don't mind. But..."

He pulled her close and ran his nose along her forehead. "I'd like that very much."

"But I feel awful. I should've had us arm ourselves with the altered candy and taken the back roads at night. I should've been more careful. I messed up during our talk with Callum, too. I always blurt things out and I wish I was more like you, so measured and smart."

"Hah. Right. I'm so even keeled. Sure."

"You do have a temper, but yes, you seem to know what to do all the time."

"I don't. Hardly ever. I'm making this up as I go along, just like you, just like all of us. And I certainly think we should firework one another while we can."

She smiled sadly, tears shining in her big eyes. "The others will be busy with the candy for at least a few minutes. I saw a quiet spot on our way in yesterday. Is there a library here?"

"Aye. Just here." He pointed to a wooden door covered in carved thistles. A likeness of Scone Palace sat below the plants' tangled roots.

Aini tugged him into the dark library. He shut the door with a foot.

His hands had a mind of their own. His palm smoothed the fabric covering Aini's hips, all the way to the stripes over her flat stomach. His thumbs stopped just below the curve of her breasts. Body thrumming with want, he closed his mouth over her lower lip and she let out a small noise that undid him. She kissed him back, her teeth nipping lightly, before her mouth moved to the spot behind his ear. A kiss there, and heat raged down him, through him, making coherent thought near impossible. His hands were in her hair then and she pulled back, her lipstick everywhere.

"Do you miss my long hair?"

"No, hen," he said, laughing, "I'd be mad for you even if you were bald as Myles."

"Please don't bring up Myles right now."

"Don't have to tell me twice." He touched his mouth to the smooth lines of her collarbone and slid his hands down her back. The feel of her body against his was too much. She was so soft and so strong. He wanted more than kisses in a library corner. "Aini. What if we—"

A knock on the door cut him off. "Sorry to interrupt, but," Neve said through the thick oak, "we're supposed to be practicing with the altered sweets, right?"

Thane squeezed his eyes shut and tried very hard not to be rude. Neve was fantastic and she didn't deserve the rough end of the chemicals currently raging through his body. "Of course, Neve. Be right there."

Aini laughed against Thane's chest. "The rest of our fireworks show will have to wait."

Thane adjusted his clothing and things. "Ugh." It wasn't as easy to switch gears with this amazing girl of his. Finally, he took Aini's hand and they left the library.

CHAPTER 14
COLORFUL TRAINING

Candies—red, purple, pink, brown, and gold—covered Aini's neatly made bed.

"Be sure about which one you want to try." She chose the golden taffy.

"Yes," Thane said, "because I truly don't think you should intake more than one type. I worry about brain damage."

Myles patted his own head. "I really don't want to risk the little I've got up there."

"No one is going pressure you, Myles. You do what you feel is best."

He smiled genuinely. "Aww, I need to do it. I don't want lovely Neve to think I'm a coward."

"Giving in to peer pressure makes you more of a feartie, darling," Neve said, picking up a chocolate drop.

"You people kill me." Vera pulled a cherry drop out of her pocket, walked up to Bran, and shoved it into his mouth.

"Vera!" Thane ran over to him and patted him on the back as he sputtered and spit the thing onto the floor.

Bran straightened and rubbed a sleeve over his mouth. "I'm fine." He nodded to Thane, then turned to Vera. "You need to stay away from me."

"What are you doing?" Aini grabbed Vera's arm and spun her around. "It is NOT OKAY to shove altered sweets down throats."

She laughed loud. "Calm down. I was just having a bit of fun with tall, dark, and handsome."

"You two have zero in common," Aini hissed in her ear. "I don't know why you think you can seduce him."

"Seer, let me have my fun."

"That is not fun," Neve said. "That is assault."

"You wouldn't know fun if it hit you in the face," Vera said to Neve.

Neve socked Vera right in the nose.

Both girls bent, howling. Neve held her hand and Vera, her nose.

Blood seeped between Vera's fingers. "You glaikit girl. So you want both boys, do you? Myles, you can have. Bran, now he will be mine before this thing is through."

"Don't I get a say in it?" Bran asked, looking pretty thunderous.

Thane examined Neve's hand. "Good thing you used your palm and not your fist. You would've broken it if you'd tried that."

"Vera!" Bran started toward her.

But Vera didn't answer. She sauntered from the room, dripping blood. She was terrible, but she was tough. They would definitely have to rein her in. Unfortunately, Aini thought that was probably her own job.

"I really, really want to call her very bad names." Neve glared at the door.

Aini couldn't agree more.

"Go right ahead, love," Myles said. "Let it flow. We support you. Better in than out. Or something."

Thane's mouth lifted as he put the remaining candies back into the containers Aini had organized. Bran said something to him that made him laugh darkly.

"All right, everyone," Aini said. "I'm going to head toward town and to find a kirkyard. I want to see if this improved Cone5 taffy helps me see spirits more readily. Anyone want to come?"

"As enticing as that is," Myles said, "I think I'd rather have a fight training sesh with Thane and Bran here. Blood before boogie men, I always say."

"Boogie men?" Thane cocked his head.

"He means ghosts." Aini headed toward the door. "All right then, have fun with some fighting. Neve, want to come along?"

"Yeah. I don't want to, but I will. For you, Seer." Wincing, Neve shook her hand. Her palm was splotchy.

"Please just call me Aini. You're my friend, not my disciple."

Neve hugged her and just about broke a rib.

"Take it easy." Aini stepped back. "Your chocolate power is dangerous."

"Och. I'm sorry." Neve covered her mouth with her hands. "I didn't mean to hurt you."

Myles sighed dramatically. "I know I'm about to hear that same phrase from Thane one thousand times."

Thane grinned like a maniac and cracked his knuckles. "It was your idea, colonial."

Aini paused by the door. "How about we watch a bout or two first?"

Neve bit her lip. "All right."

Myles shrieked and ran at Thane, one hand raised like he could hammer Thane into the floor somehow. Thane caught

Myles's forearm, stuck out a foot, and Myles landed in a heap at the foot of Aini's bed. Bran put a shin across Myles's stomach, his other leg extended for balance.

"Don't show me what you're trying, colonial," Thane said.

"Don't break my back in the learning process, Lord Heir."

Bran helped Myles up. "Keep your hands up, near your face, to protect yourself. Don't look where you're about to strike. Don't hesitate."

"And less screaming would be good," Aini added.

"Aye," Neve said, "but did you know when ancient Highlanders went into battle, they often shrieked wildly to throw their enemy off?" She raised both eyebrows like this was the most exciting thing ever.

Bran tilted his head toward Neve. "She's right."

"That is interesting," Aini said, giving Neve an indulgent smile.

Myles threw a punch, and Thane pushed it off to the side, past his ear. "That's called a parry. Doesn't need to be much, just a wee shove."

Thane began throwing slow punches at Myles's chin. Myles used the parry to keep from getting hit.

"Good job!" Neve clapped once, grimaced at her palm, then rested her hands gingerly on her hips.

A sheen of sweat made Thane's cheeks and forehead shine. His undershirt stuck to the planes of his chest and the curve of his upper arms and shoulders. "Now we'll go the ground and I'll teach you how to sweep a man off you."

"Or a woman," Aini said. Then she blushed realizing how this sounded.

"I need to practice that one," Bran said, an eye on the door, watching for Vera's return. "Or maybe I don't since Neve Breaker-of-Bones Moore is around."

Myles covered his heart with his hands. "Breaker-of-hearts."

Bran and Myles traded a look that said they might have a bit too much in common in the way of Neve.

Myles's mouth switched from grin to glare. "I had her first, you handsome Scottish devil. And I make her laugh."

"I won't take her from you, lad," Bran said gently.

Aini was so glad Thane had Bran in his life. With all the horror he'd endured, Thane needed a good friend like Bran. Myles did too.

The boys began to tussle again, sweating and laughing as they threw punches and tossed one another onto the floor.

"Let's let them have their fun," Aini said, checking to be sure she had the golden taffy wrapped well. "They should enjoy some laughs while they can."

A FAIRLY NICE DAY TURNED INTO AN ICY, FOGGY ONE AS AINI and Neve passed the first of the gravestones.

"Why did I agree to this?" Neve tugged her sweater so it came right up under her chin.

"Because you're the best friend I've ever had."

Neve squeezed Aini's arm gently, using just her fingertips.

"Appreciated," Aini said.

With the effects of the taffy fully in play, the fog's white plumes took on more color. A pale, iridescent green shifted through the air and wove into a deep wine color that moved more slowly. Aini waved a hand through the myriad of colors.

"I wonder what all this really is."

"What is?"

"The colors I'm seeing. There is this green and a burgundy... is it gases in the air or what?"

"I have no idea. That's a question for Thane."

Then they had no more time for speculating because a human shape was forming not ten feet from where they stood. Over a head-high grave marker of an angel, a ghost shimmered into view. The blue-white light that had been around the ghost kings and Lady Greensleeves was nowhere to be seen. Instead, the air around the vague shape shimmered a color Aini had no name for.

"Can you see that?" Aini pointed.

Neve shivered. "No. Is it a spirit?"

"I think so. But it doesn't have that same color."

"The kind of light the kings had?"

"Right."

The unnameable hue faded and the bluish white light replaced it. Neve gasped.

"Ah. There's that color they usually have," Aini said.

The ghost drifted closer, the colored fog stirring around his bulky frame. "Do not come here." His eyes darkened.

"We need to get out of here." Aini snagged Neve's hand and they ran to the far side of the kirkyard.

Another ghost materialized near a snowdrift by the kirkyard's stone wall. With the Cone5 working, Aini saw it first and pulled Neve to a halt before they could sprint straight through him. This former person wore clothing from at least two hundred years ago. A patch covered his right eye.

"It's another one," Aini said as the blue-white light that would allow Neve to see bloomed into being.

Neve gave a single nod and seemed to gather herself up. "You should ask him about the earl and see if he has any suggestions on how to sway him."

The spirit spoke before Aini could say a word. "Command me, Seer."

A shudder danced through Aini's ribcage. "Who are you?"

"A salmon trader's son." His words wavered, fading in and out, making it nearly impossible to understand. "...your strength...could call one such as me without the Coronation Stone."

Aini's heart lurched. "What did you say? What do you mean?"

He inclined his head. The scent of the river—wet banks and minerals in the water—rose off his glimmering form. "I am no king. I come because you are the Seer."

"What is he saying?"

Neve leaned closer as if proximity were the reason she couldn't understand the spirit's words. Of course that wasn't true, but this ghost did seem more human than any of the others they'd run into so it made sense Neve's first reaction was to come close to hear him like she would a person who was speaking softly.

"I can command you even though the Heir isn't here with the stone?"

The ghost nodded. "I am no king."

Aini turned to Neve. "I think this boy is willing to do what I ask because he somehow knows I am the Seer."

"Could he fight for us?"

The spirit lifted, then fell, his shoes dipping into the earth. Aini felt desperate to squeeze information from him before he faded away. "Can you fight?"

Confusion twisted his face. "Touch? No. I am no king."

"I don't think he can physically affect the living world," Aini said to Neve.

"What about a message?" Neve jerked her chin back toward the castle. "Maybe he could persuade the earl to make a decision we like."

"Would you do that?" Aini asked the spirit. "Can you tell Earl

Callum to support the rebellion against Earl Nathair, Chief of Clan Campbell and the king's Head of Security?" She felt the odd need to be formal with this boy.

"As you will it, Seer." The ghost's form exploded into a shower of glittering dust and the kirkyard fell silent. The click of the icy rain on the tombstones was the only sound.

"He is going to talk to Callum," Aini said. That was unexpected.

"What if he threatens the earl?" Neve walked at Aini's elbow. The heavy fog still shrouded the kirkyard's entrance.

"I hope it doesn't come to that, but if it does, well...it'll be for a good cause."

AINI FOUND THANE IN THE DINING ROOM WHERE HE WAS scribbling on a piece of paper. Numbers and letters filled every inch of the sheet except for one spot where he'd sketched a brain coded with patterns that showed which altered sweets affected which region.

He mumbled under his breath and pushed up glasses that weren't there. "Scandium, Titanium, Vanadium, Chromium, Manganese..." A smile lifted Aini's cheeks. He was rattling off the periodic table of elements.

She put a hand on his shoulder, feeling the muscles under his shirt, warm and strong. He hadn't donned that terrible sweater yet because Callum's staff had taken most of their clothes to be laundered and given each a spare set of something simple to wear. "It's going to be okay. I found another ally for us in the kirkyard."

Turning, he looked up at her with wide eyes.

She told him about the salmon fisherman's son and the effects of the Cone5.

"I wonder if it'll work."

Callum strode into the room, boots covered in grass clippings and his face pale. "I'll help you, lad. Lassie. It'll be an awful mess, but I'm in it with you. To the end."

Aini longed to ask if the ghost's message was what had moved him to this decision, but she didn't want to push it. Too often lately, she'd blurted things out and acted rashly. Bravery was one thing, but she'd gone past that a time or ten and sailed right into foolishness. She had to regain her strong practical instincts and be smart about what she suggested, said, and did.

"Are you truly ready to rebel against your father and your king, young Thane? How about you, Seer? Are you prepared to go to your deaths if the chaos calls for it?" As Callum spoke, Myles, Vera, Neve, and Bran walked into the room.

Thane stood. "I thank you for siding with us, Uncle Callum. And yes, I am ready. As ready as I'll ever be."

"It's not as if we have much of a choice," Aini said. "We're called to do this and fate won't let us ignore the situation at hand."

"Yeah the baddies are going after you all regardless, so you might as well give them some good trouble," Myles said.

Thane cracked a smile, but Callum's face remained serious.

"What do you suggest we do first?" Callum asked. The butler/guard/server came in with a tea tray and Callum waved the man out of the room.

"Will you call a clan gathering at Inveraray for me, Uncle?" Thane's jaw cast a shadow over the tendons in his neck and the worn edge of his white undershirt.

"You're certain that's the right choice."

"I must detail Nathair's and the king's wrongdoings. Then we'll expose who we are and what we plan to do." He nodded toward Aini. "I have to make my plea, answer their questions, and win them to our side."

Callum smiled sadly. "Aye. To do this and come out alive, you will need to do a great deal of very fine talking."

"As long as I don't have to jump any more of your bonfires, I'll be fine."

Callum barked a laugh. "I can't promise you that won't happen after a few drams of whisky."

Relief loosened Aini's tensed muscles and relaxed her fists. The revolution was about to begin in earnest, but at least they had this powerful earl to back them.

CHAPTER 15
A CALLING OF THE CLANS

Thane had only seen it done three times. Never from here. Uncle Callum put five of his loyal men and women onto horses. The saddles bore skirts showing his coat of arms, and as the riders burst from the front gates of Huntingtower, the colored fabric fluttered in the vortex of the horses' speed and the opposing wind. Hooves threw chunks of grass and soil behind the mounts and Callum blew a horn taken from a Highland cow. The sound reverberated in Thane's chest and reminded him of the kings' blood inside his veins.

Thane stood close to his uncle, near enough to smell his shaving cream and the wet wool of his coat. No one in his family, extended or immediate, had ever risked this much for him.

"I thank you, Uncle," he said softly, feeling very young. "If there's anything I can do..."

"You can win, that's what you can do. Win, then let me come back here, to my home and my people."

The beat of hooves faded as Aini drew up beside Thane. "Why horses and not cars?"

"It's tradition," Thane said. "No other news is delivered this way. Only the call for a gathering. The moment the horses are spotted in each county, word is spread and the traveling begins. It won't take nearly as long as you might guess." He faced her and set his hands on her shoulders. "Are you ready to stop doubting yourself and act as the Seer that you are?"

Smirking, she covered his hands with hers. "Say that into a mirror, love."

He pursed his lips and nodded. "Are *we* ready?"

She studied the space around him, most likely watching his aura glow. "I know one thing for sure."

"What's that?"

"I am more than ready to stop sneaking around in dirty boots, pretending to be someone else."

"Is it the pretending or the unclean footwear that has you most bothered?"

"Shut your gob, laddie." Aini pinched his stomach and marched back inside.

Thane said a little prayer that she would make it through this. It would kill him if she...no, he wouldn't say it. Not even in his mind.

THE LATE AFTERNOON SUN WARMED THE STEERING WHEEL AND Thane's knuckles. The road was empty. Too empty. He didn't want to mention it and worry the group more as they approached Inveraray. The quiet back roads gave way to salt-white shops, black roofs, and...gray pavement devoid of any tourists or locals? A dark feeling crawled down Thane's back.

"Do you have your taffy on you?" he asked Aini.

She'd told him the young ghost claimed she could command

him and other lesser ghosts. Hopefully, they'd scare the stuff out of their enemies.

"Yes. Do you have your caramel?"

"Aye. But no gun."

"Well, we agreed on no obvious weapons, right?"

"Right," Bran said from the backseat.

Myles snorted. "Besides the caravan of Callum and company behind us who are surely toting buckets of guns."

"Yes, besides that, we come in peace." Aini's lips bunched to one side like she was thinking.

Thane's palms began to sweat. "I never took the stone from its hidey hole in the back of the truck." He lowered the visor to block the harsh, lowering sun. "How am I supposed to do anything with that big boy anyway?"

"I really want to make a joke right now," Myles said.

Neve tsked at him. "Restrain yourself."

"It's a valid question," Bran said.

"You commanded that ghost to talk Callum into his decision," Neve said. "So why do we need the stone now? Aside from making it roar in front of the people to show them you're the Heir."

Aini shook her head. "The ghost I used to send the message to Callum said he couldn't do anything physical to this world. It's my guess that only the ghost kings can carry out any true defense of the Heir. We need the stone in Thane's hands to call them up."

"Which leads back to my question: how do I use the stone properly? It's no small rock."

Aini snapped her fingers and some of Thane's worry faded at the sight of her mind at work. "We can break off another piece of the stone. A small piece. You could wear it on a chain around your neck."

"Och, that's a braw plan," Bran said. "Does anyone have a drill in their back pocket?"

"Are you being sarcastic with our Seer?" Vera hadn't spoken since the nose-breaking. Thane had hoped she was working toward being amenable. But maybe she was merely angry as a wet cat. "You can slight me all you like, you and your bizarre threesome you have going on back there." She looked at Myles and Neve in turn. "But the Dionadair won't put up with you disrespecting our Seer."

"I meant no disrespect at all."

Bran's voice was dangerous. He may have been the kindest man Thane knew, besides Lewis MacGregor, but he had beaten deadlier people than Vera down, and Thane had no doubt he'd take the whole rebel crew on if he thought it was the right thing to do.

Thane blinked at the sun and took a right turn. "We'll stop at the car park just there, near the apothecary, and see if Callum's group has a way to make this chip of the stone."

A HALF HOUR LATER THANE WORE A LEATHER STRING AROUND his neck. A chunk of the Coronation Stone, roughly the size of a pound sterling, hung heavily from a metal ring. Bran had drilled the tiny, careful hole, using his explosives skills. Thane kept the stone between his undershirt and his sweater, not wanting the magical object to touch his skin.

"Does it feel strange?" Aini asked as they started toward home.

"It does." The fire in his blood burned hotter with the stone so close to his flesh. It was a scary sensation. Like he might come undone if he kept it so close for too long.

"Your aura is brighter. What are you worrying about?" She

squeezed against him to look in the mirror at the trail of trucks and cars behind them, probably double-checking Callum was keeping his word.

"Not about my uncle, if that's your fear. I've never seen him break his word. I don't like the look of the streets, if I'm honest."

"There's not a person out today," Neve said, "and with this better weather, you'd think they'd be at the shops." She spoke the truth. After all that rain and ice, folk should've been on the streets, buying and talking and drinking.

Everyone in the truck went quiet as they drove past a sign for the castle.

"I've never seen Inveraray Castle." Aini leaned over Thane's arm to peer out the window as he turned the truck toward the new gatehouse at the base of the drive.

A woman and a man in Campbell tartan and kingsmen jackets stood at the barred entrance. Codekeepers. Thane's pulse ticked faster. Faster. This was the moment. They'd be shot on sight if Nathair had found out about Bass Rock and the death of Rodric.

Thane lowered the window. "Gallowglass," he said.

Aini shared a puzzled look with Myles. Thankfully, both kept quiet.

The woman pressed a button and the black, iron gates swung open.

The pebbled drive curved between hedges that threw dark green shadows. The flickering shapes of birds shook the tiny leaves, making the plants themselves seem nervous.

Vera cleared her throat noisily. "I just hope you have the stones to lead, Heir."

Maybe it was just the stress of everything, but Thane was

fairly certain Vera was growing meaner by the day. Thane threw the door open and Aini climbed out behind him.

"Stones the lad has," Bran said. "It's his sense of self-preservation I'm not so very certain about."

The group cleared the truck to catch the first view of Thane's childhood home.

Aini sucked in a breath.

Thane tried to see it as Aini would. Larger than Huntingtower. Less ancient, more majestic. The structure blocked the orange-pink glow of the setting sun. Its smooth, stone exterior had a corpse's pallor. A series of conical towers, graced with medieval style turrets, stood guard at the ends. Gothic, arched windows looked down on the group. The newer stone surrounded what looked like an older, more square version of what castles started out as—fortifications. Part of this house was very old. Part of it was much less ancient.

"Can you see the old keep within the structure?" Neve said.

"I noticed that." Aini just kept staring.

Whistling low, Myles took Neve's arm and followed Thane. "Let's hope we live long enough to show this place our backsides as we leave."

"From your lips to God's ears," Neve said.

Thane's took a breath and tried to calm down as he surveyed his childhood home. He could not drown in that overwhelmed feeling right now. "Welcome to Inveraray Castle, everyone," he said darkly.

Vera fluffed her short dress and fell into line behind Aini.

Bran looked like he was about to vomit. Made sense. He'd seen more of what Clan Campbell could do than the rest of them combined, save Thane.

CHAPTER 16
DEMONS TO WRESTLE

No kingsmen guards in Campbell colors flanked the door. Aini wasn't sure that was good. A woman with white hair piled high on her head and a long woolen skirt emerged from the front door. Something about the set of her shoulders and the shape of her head reminded Aini of Thane.

Thane's face softened as the woman smiled at him. "What happened to your phone? And where is Jimmy?"

The woman squeezed her eyes shut and pressed her fingers tightly against the back of his neck. Her skin was smooth for someone with white hair, her face nearly free of lines. Why would a woman of her age—perhaps a little younger than Aini's father—have lost all the color in her hair?

"Oh I'll tell you everything, but first let me meet your friends." A shadow crossed her face. It could've been fear or worry, or maybe she had a secret.

Thane hugged her again, then presented his mother to Aini and the others. "This is my dear mother, Senga Campbell."

"I knew it," Vera whispered. "Maternal threads are a very peculiar shade. I'm getting better at this every day."

Aini put her hands over her heart. Her own mother would never meet him. Her eyes burned. At least her mother wasn't suffering through this.

"Welcome." Senga's voice was a little shaky, like she was nervous. She touched her silver ball earrings nervously and opened the door. "Please come inside."

The group gathered awkwardly under the chandelier of the entry hall as Thane took his mother aside.

"Have you heard any talk about me?" he asked her.

"You know no one tells me much of anything."

"I also know you have your way of finding out what you need to know."

"Not any more. Your father lies and lies and all anyone around here does is parrot him."

She led everyone into a mint-colored parlor covered from ceiling to floor in tapestries.

"Two days ago, one of the guards took my phone. No one will admit it, but I had it next to me while I was reading the paper. A woman came in to retrieve something from Nathair's desk, then the phone was gone. It was her. I know it. But why, I have no idea. And Jimmy. He disappeared."

"When did you see him last? Was there an argument?"

"Who is Jimmy, if I may ask?" If he was Thane's brother, surely Aini would've heard about him before now.

Thane swallowed. "Jimmy is our butler. He has run the household for more than three years now. He's a good sort."

Senga agreed. "I've told the kingsmen here to look for him, to ask after his family in Inverness, but we haven't heard anything."

"Probably wise of him to fly the coop before the foxes get hungry."

"What do you mean, son? Are you in some trouble?"

"The streets are empty, Mother. Have you been out today? No one is around."

Aini hated the stress in his voice. She wished she could take him away from all this or annihilate those who caused him pain. But that person was his own father. Her stomach rolled. To have that kind of man as a father. She thanked God his mother seemed like a good person.

Thane went on. "Has there been some sort of announcement or a curfew or something?"

"Not that I know of," Senga said.

"I have a great deal to tell you." Thane touched the spot where the piece of the stone rested under his sweater. "First, you should know that Uncle Callum's entire retinue is here, just outside the main gates."

Senga lowered her gaze on Thane. "Start at the beginning of your story."

And so he did, with some moments filled in by Aini and the rest.

THE LONGEST HALF HOUR IN THE HISTORY OF THE WORLD passed finally. How could Senga possibly believe all of this madness?

Senga looked at Vera. "You are Dionadair?"

A grin tugged at Aini's mouth. Senga trusted them.

"Aye," Vera said. "And I hope you'll join us and become a rebel too."

Senga rubbed a spot between her eyebrows and went to the

window. Then, as if what they'd told her had finally sunk in, she hurried over to Thane and grabbed him, pulling him into her arms. She said something to him and he patted her back.

"It'll be all right," he said quietly.

He gave her a smile, and Aini could see the little boy he used to be, all blue eyes and bright hope. Hope Nathair had all but ruined. Anger at the Earl of Argyll burned inside her, and it was all she could do not to rage around the room, destroying everything the man had touched.

"Are you all right, Aini?" Neve touched her knee.

"Yes. Sorry. Yes."

"Of course I'll do whatever I can to aid you." Unshed tears glistened in Senga's wise eyes. "It's long past time I stood up for myself and for you." She pressed two fingers against her forehead. "I've been a terrible mother." With a deep breath, she regained her composure and waved off Thane's and Bran's attempts to comfort her. "I'm fine. It does no good to wallow in self-pity. We have work to do. First, we must bring Callum in, have a meeting, then we'll set you up in your Campbell tartan and have you fully look the part of the true chief of Clan Campbell. I must say I am very glad to have Callum here and on our side of things. My sister would've been proud. She always hated Nathair. I should've listened to her when she warned me of his angry streak on our wedding day."

Aini couldn't stop herself from getting up and throwing her arms around Senga. "I hope this is okay."

Senga's shining eyes were the same color as Thane's. "Where did he find you?"

"In a lab."

Senga laughed. "Of course he did. Thane, do you know how lucky you are?"

Thane did a double-take. "How did you even know we're together?"

Vera and Neve said in unison, "Please." Then they glared at one another.

"It's obvious, my dear," Senga said to Thane, who'd adorably gone a little red around the ears.

AINI LAY IN A CURTAINED BED IN THE CASTLE OF THE MOST powerful family in Scotland. She was dating the son of said family. He was about to overthrow the entire clan.

How in the world had she come into this situation?

Sweat pricked at her forehead as she got up to dress. The world was spinning too fast. She hadn't slept a wink last night. It wasn't the different smells of Inveraray—those were nice. Roses, wood polish, evergreens. The lack of noise didn't hurt her state of mind either although it was odd to not hear Neve lightly snoring or the lorries squeaking by like they did at all hours back in Edinburgh. No, she hadn't slept because two hundred and sixty, give or take, clan representatives and every adult member of Clan Campbell were currently driving sports cars, utility vehicles, and probably, horses directly to this very spot. *Insane.* Aini put a hand on the cold sink in the room's private bath. These men and women, of the Highlands mostly, would either raise Aini and Thane up to lead, or rip them down and feed them to Nathair.

Aini brushed her teeth and flossed twice because it made life feel better somehow.

At least the meeting with Callum had gone smoothly. That was a good start, a good omen perhaps. He'd even apologized to Aini, Thane, and Vera for his comments against sixth-sensers.

When Senga brought up her deceased sister, Callum had

given out another apology—this one to Senga for not looking into her well-being here at Inveraray more recently. He knew exactly how Nathair was and he claimed he should've done more to help her escape. He admitted to fear for himself and his county. After promising every weapon, resource, and able-bodied and willing man and woman of Perthshire to this new cause, he'd bent the knee to Thane and sworn fealty. Thane had jerked the man back up though, telling him it wasn't official, so Callum shouldn't swear yet. Thane had to first receive approval from the leading members of Clan Campbell, then they could move on to gaining fealty from other clans such as Callum's. So far, this venture was looking up.

But Aini's nerves couldn't feel the optimism that her practical mind wanted them to. They just kept vibrating and itching and pulling her thoughts apart so she had trouble remembering whether she'd told everyone she needed to tell something to.

Wearing the blue and brown short dress Senga magically drummed up for her, she found everyone else downstairs where breakfast had obviously started long ago. Usually, Aini was the one making breakfast, or at least the one of the first in the group to get out of bed. Not today. Today, she'd hidden behind those bed curtains and ignored the sunrise, her mind dizzy.

Neve handed her a blueberry scone wrapped in a linen napkin. "I actually thought you'd died."

"I bet the sun tried to go back down this morning because it thought something was wrong with Aini not buzzing around." Myles poured her a cup of coffee.

Thane took the coffee and handed it to Aini.

Sun poured through the windows and turned Thane's hair to gold.

"Your hair isn't black," she stammered. It wasn't what they

needed to discuss on this most important day, but the words just poured right out of her mouth.

Thane grinned with one side of his mouth and her stomach flipped pleasantly. "No, hen. I had it dyed back last night. I need to look like who I am now. Well, except for the glasses. Those are far away and will have to wait. Thankfully, my prescription isn't so bad."

Aini wiggled her feet which were now, thank the stars above, wearing clean black flats. "I didn't get rid of the purple," she pointed to her hair, "but at least my feet feel like my feet again. Those old boots..." She shuddered. It was one thing to deal with dirt you'd earned on your own adventures, but someone else's dirt? Too much.

"I'm sticking with the blond for now," Neve said, tossing her hair over her shoulder awkwardly and making Myles snicker. "It's completely me."

"I can grab our stylist to fix that if you'd like," Thane said.

"Our stylist." Myles slapped a knee. "You are too much."

"Oh as if you lived in squalor back in the colonies on your multi-millions worth plantation," Thane said.

"We did not have a stylist."

"The Campbells have one because Nathair has to make public appearances. It's part of his job."

Myles's eyes went wide. "Did you just defend Nathair Campbell?"

"I defended the Campbells."

"I guess that's something we're going to start doing," Aini said.

Bran took a loud sip of coffee, then refilled the cup before the attendant could get to it. "Thane will lead the clan, and we'll be sided up with them."

Vera's hand went to her stomach. "I'm going to boak."

"I'm used to backing them as needed," Bran said.

"Why did you always stick with me, Bran?" Thane sat back while the household staff cleared his plate and Bran's beside him.

"Because you stuck with me. I love you, lad."

Thane winked. "And I you, friend."

"No really. You're my only friend and you saved me from my own natural inclination toward self-pity."

"This is just beautiful." Myles leaned back in his chair and propped a knee against the table's edge.

"I didn't know you were having problems when I met you, Bran." Thane touched the rim of his coffee cup and stared into the black drink. "You seemed to have it all together. You made a killing tending bar up here. You had a smile for everyone."

"And I wanted to off myself every single night. Until I met you and you needed me."

"I needed you?"

"You did. You still do. You always will. I see your dark spots, have lived with you through the dark places, and will launch into more darkness until one of us stops breathing. You were a boy with a golden heart. Now, you're a man I can follow instead of lead. It's a relief, really. I've done well."

"You sound like his daddy." Myles raised his eyebrows. "Doesn't he?" He nudged Aini.

"Yes. I do think Bran served Thane in ways Nathair never could."

"And at times when I couldn't," Senga said as she walked in, a small, white dog at her heels. "I couldn't trail you like Bran. I also had my own demons to wrestle."

"You are the best mother a man could have." Thane stood and pulled a chair out for her.

Aini melted. "When you're finished here, Thane, would you

meet me in the gardens out back? If you think we have time before the representatives get here that is."

"You have time." Senga said something to an attendant who set a plate in front of her. "Go on, Aini. Just allow me a moment with my son first."

"Of course." Aini gave Neve a brief hug and found the door to the outside.

CHAPTER 17
AMONG THE TWISTED VINES

Under rolling clouds, Thane strode around the side of the castle and searched for Aini. Myles had tipped him off that she'd gone in search of a quiet place to take a breath but hadn't taken a car into town or anything. She just wanted some time away from the arguments and discussions about what might happen when the clan representatives arrived. Thane couldn't blame her. It'd been a wild few hours, and she had to be thinking of her father back at the safe house and wondering if he was truly safe.

He wasn't. None of them were.

He found Aini leaning against the pointed arches of the southwest bridge, her form tiny under the frame of solid stone. A lock of her hair had escaped and blew the way she was looking, toward the snow-touched vines of the sleepy garden and the low hills beyond.

She has so much more than shallow beauty. A sharp mind within and a brave heart beating in her chest.

With a silent prayer that she would still want him after all of this, despite what he'd done during his time with Nathair, Thane approached her. At least she didn't know every crime. If she learned what he'd done to persuade Rodric to include him in the operation on Bass Rock, she'd never speak to him again. Even if it was truly the one way he could've been there, in that position, to help Aini and the Dionadair survive that night.

As always, Thane wrestled the horrible memory down, then buried the blood and guilt in the farthest reaches of his mind, and tried to remember who he wanted to be, not who he'd had to be all these years. He started toward Aini again, his heart drumming an uneven tattoo on his ribcage.

She didn't look up as he walked up and touched her on the back. Her skin was warm under her dark blue short dress. The brown stripes in the fabric matched her eyes.

Maybe she'd come to her senses and decided not to be with him. He wouldn't blame her a bit. "Do you wish I'd leave you alone?"

A smile pulled at those full, plum lips of hers. "No," she said, staring at frozen spots in the evergreens spilling over the earthen walls. Her flats crunched the gravel as she adjusted her weight away from the arch. "Is this going to work? Will Callum's support be enough?"

Thane swallowed. "There's no way to know. I think maybe that's not what you really want to say."

She spun to face him. "Should we get your mother away from here? Just in case this all goes badly? If she has to lose you, right in front of her..."

"So you think I'll be shot down the moment everyone arrives, aye?"

"That's not what I meant. I just don't want her to suffer. She has been through so much."

"And we should tuck her away safely, hm?"

"She would hate that. She wouldn't go."

"No, she wouldn't. You're a bit like her, you know."

Aini smiled. "I should be so lucky."

"Thank you for coming here. For risking everything."

"I'm still amazed you put me up as leader of the rebellion." Her eyes were so dark they were nearly black. Like the peat water in the lochs. "There aren't too many people who would give up the chance to rule it all."

He frowned at her. Her eyes were open and true. What did she mean? He'd done it because they were a team and he wanted to do everything with her at his side if she willed it.

"You could've claimed all that power for yourself," she said. "You know you're the Heir, but you don't care about that part of it, do you?"

Not after the life he'd had and what he'd seen of power in one man's hands. He shook his head. "I only want us all to be free of my father."

"What made you decide this is what you wanted to do, to claim your right and fight Nathair?"

The fire in her eyes, the strength he'd seen that had made him want to destroy his father and all the man had created, was still there in the brown-black depths. It was quiet now, smoldering, but still there.

"You."

He brought her fingers to his lips. Her lids, slightly purple at their edges, pressed together and a single tear escaped each one. If only he could take her away from all this and escape to the quiet of the Highlands. They could find peace in a wee house with nothing to do but mind the sheep and make love. Not necessarily in that order.

"It'll be over soon. For good or bad. It'll be over." He kissed her fingers. They were soft and light and smelled like the herbs and grasses she touched in passing.

Through her thick lashes, she looked up at him. It was like his body had a burning thirst and only her touch could quench it. He clapped a hand around her waist and crushed her sweet mouth with his. She made a little noise, and his chest heaved with wanting her as he eased into the kiss. Her arms circled his neck, and he ran his lips along her warm throat. As they fell against the arch, his entire body—from the tip of his head to the toes in his boots—sparked and burned.

"They'll be here soon," he said. "I should stop."

She grabbed his coat and whirled them both around to bump against the arch. "Oh no you shouldn't." She kissed him firmly. A punch of desire hit him. "If we have to deal with the pain of this world," she said against his lips, "we get to enjoy the perks of it too. I'm pretty sure you said that first."

He grinned. "How can I argue with you, my Merlin?"

"You can't. Now shut up and kiss me," she said, and he did.

When he knew they had to stop or risk moving into something she might not be ready for, he found a bench for them. While Vera, Bran, Callum, and the rest worked on forming the best arguments to win over Clan Campbell and those clans loyal to Campbell, Thane and Aini told jokes Myles had taught them and made up stories about each of the sheep on the hill.

CHAPTER 18
WITH A SHOUT AND A TURN

A riot of rumbling engines, loud voices, and an explosion of ravens soaring into the snow-gray sky tore Thane's attention from Aini's troubled face.

A gun fired.

They traded a confused look, then ran toward the shouting.

In the drive in front of Thane's insanely large childhood home, two armies had assembled.

Callum bellowed over his group of currently unarmed men and women from Perthshire toward a group of newcomers. "Calm yourselves. I called a gathering to talk and that talk includes why there is a disguised Dionadair truck alongside my vehicles. I wouldn't call you if there wasn't a very good reason. We need to listen to Thane and his group here. They have information vital to Scotland's well-being. To its future."

"How did they know the truck belonged to Owen and the rest?" Aini craned her neck to look at the truck they'd come in.

The rebels had painted it just before the group had left the safe house. It bore no telltale gunshot wounds or the bright blue color the rebels sometimes painted on bridges and roads.

Thane shrugged, eyes narrowing behind his glasses. "I'm sure they'd have changed the plates." He should've made certain.

Menzies—the very cousin he'd warned everyone about—raised his crooked nose and waved a gun at Thane. "Here is the man of the day. I know full well you're the one who put Callum up to this gathering. You think you can show up here with people we've never seen before," he gestured toward Vera and Aini, "and suddenly we're at your feet? Earl Nathair may've gone off the map, but we're not desperate enough to need you and your wild ideas, whelp."

"We're not desperate at all," a man in Campbell tartan said.

"Earl Nathair hasn't disappeared," a red-cheeked woman said. "He is just on the job, man. Watch yourself. Don't go calling our chief's son a whelp, Menzies."

"Aye," another agreed. "Go easy. That's the earl's son, remember."

More voices joined in to defend Thane, but it wasn't exactly what he needed them to feel. "Thane is the heir to Clan Campbell and fights as well as his grandsire once did."

"Menzies," Callum said darkly. "You know me. Do you think I'd call a gathering just for the giggles?"

"And I thought you had brains enough not to pull something like this. Ah. I'm seeing it now." Menzies rubbed his chin. "You want to move the lad around like your puppet. You want control. You know you should be content enough that the king forgave the Gowries for their bitter past and enjoy the lands you have."

Mother walked down the front steps and it was all Thane could do not to run to her and push her back inside the house. "That's some fealty you're showing there, Menzies," she said.

Menzies glared her way. "Stay out of this, Senga, and there

won't be a need for too much violence. I'm just trying to teach your son here the lessons you failed to."

Anger seared its way down Thane's fingers and his hands became fists.

Senga crossed her arms, her voice carrying. "Did you or did you not bend the knee to Clan Campbell, offer the hilt of your family sword, and swear to be loyal to our cause?"

Thane remembered this was how she used to look all the time—confident, tall, sharp.

"You think this falls in line with that oath?" Menzies snapped, looking flushed despite his barking tone. "You're attempting to yank your father's role as chief from under his boots."

"I want to put it to a vote," Thane said. "The representatives, yourself included, will decide that. I will accept the outcome, whatever that may be."

"Well, I won't." He pointed the gun at Aini and Thane's heart stopped. "Have you told these disciples of yours what you did to gain back Rodric's trust, Thane?"

Thane shut his eyes. He couldn't tell them. Aini would never forgive him. It had been necessary. But it was a horror—committed after he knew better than to ignore his conscience and do as Nathair and Rodric demanded—and Aini could not find out.

"Och, I can tell you have not." Menzies laughed, an ugly sound that pebbled Thane's flesh. "Let me take you down that road, will you? I'll enjoy that. What do you think? Are you his whore, you pretty little thing? Did you realize you were bedding a man who cares so little for human life? For the pain he inflicts on others?"

Aini stepped forward, eyes on fire. "I'm no whore. And I know exactly who and what Thane is."

Thane's stomach lurched. He remembered bone and blood. Lies and pain. It had nearly been the end of him.

Menzies watched Aini like the threat she was. His thumb rose over the gun's hammer and he clicked it into place, leveling the barrel for a clean shot.

Thane's whole body buzzed. "Wait. Just listen." He forced himself not to run, not to panic, not to rush Menzies' finger into pulling the trigger.

"Seer!" Vera, paled and panicking, hopped onto the bumper of the Dionadair truck, ignoring the weapons aimed at her head and staring at Aini. She ripped her sleeve. A phone was strapped to her arm. Pressing a button, she shouted, "Aini MacGregor, MacBeth's Seer, needs our help to defeat a man named Menzies!" Thane couldn't breathe as she turned to glare at Menzies. "Now the entire Dionadair are headed here with your name on their blades."

Menzies swore. "Seer, aye. I know exactly what that title entails. Allow me to put you out of your misery, traitorous abomination."

Thane pushed away from Bran, who held his sleeve, and two women he didn't know. He had to get between them. His heart and lungs shook inside his chest, threatening to pierce right through him.

He reached under his sweater and clasped the Coronation Stone.

The world shivered. The fire in Thane's blood raged hot. A blue-white light appeared around him, a circle of what he knew would form into mantles, swords, helms, and bearded kings of old. There were gasps. Shouts. The rattle of a gun hitting the drive.

Menzies eyes were big as moons. "What am I seeing?"

Thane released his hold on the stone. The light faded.

Callum picked up Menzies' gun. "I told you I wouldn't call a gathering unless I had good reason, man."

Thane put his hands on his knees and tried to breathe, watching Aini talk to Neve, unhurt, alive. The house behind her tilted. He took another breath. That gun. That was too close. He was going to kill Menzies. Someday. Somehow. Or at least keep the man from ever holding a weapon again.

The memory of what Thane had done to gain Rodric's and Nathair's trust flashed through his mind. Aini would ask about what Thane had done, what Menzies was talking about. And there the thing growing between them would die.

The clan representatives along with what appeared to be most of Clan Campbell worked their way into the house under Mother's direction. She ordered all guns and ceremonial swords onto three tables the kitchen staff had produced at the base of the front steps. Two cooks in aprons watched over the dangerous collection.

"Just in case a foul plan sneaks into your heads," Mother said, as the crowd nodded respectfully to her and streamed under the arched lintel.

Aini found Thane's side. Her mouth leaked a little blood. She must've bitten the inside of her cheek too hard. "I need to know." She crossed her arms and locked him down with her MacGregor eyebrow.

Thane was definitely going to be sick. "Please don't ask me to tell you."

"I thought we were building a relationship on trust. After the whole spying-on-me-and-my-father thing, I'd have thought you'd be keen on honesty between us."

"I am. I know. But this..."

Vera, Myles, Bran, and Neve closed a circle around them.

"You all right, pal?" Bran cocked his head.

"Aye. No. Well..." Thane rubbed his face harshly. "You don't understand, Aini."

"Make her understand," Neve said.

Myles shook his head like a fly was in his ear. "Why do we need to know really? Hasn't there been enough of this? Nathair is an arse and he messed with Thane. We know that. Why are you torturing him and making him drag out the past?"

"This isn't the past. This happened less than a week ago. After Thane had come to his senses about what his father was and what was wrong and what was right. Whatever he did, it wasn't under the influence of brainwashing."

Vera shoved into the center of the ring. "Oh, you think it's like that, aye? Know so much about it, do you, Seer?"

Thane hated Vera's tone. "Vera. Don't."

"No, I suppose I'm not aware of everything to do with brain-washing," Aini said, face open. "But I need to understand this if I'm going to risk my life, yours, my father's, as well as Scotland's future, on his ethics."

Vera laughed and held her stomach. "Forgive me, Seer, but don't think for a second that those with what you think are *proper ethics* are the ones who can run a country."

Bran coughed. "I hate to say it, but she has a good point."

Vera gave him a nod. "To beat the baddies, you must some-times become one."

"Then just tell me, Thane. Tell us what you did so we can understand."

Aini's brown eyes swallowed him up. God, he loved her so much. The way she opened herself to criticism. How she accepted new realities with such courage. The sharp mind she paired with a good, strong heart. He owed her this truth. Even if it tore them, and the rebellion apart.

He pictured that night. The fog and the sea. Rodric's mocking looks as Thane approached, hands open, weaponless.

"I'm surprised they didn't fire away the moment I walked up," he said. "Rodric was primed for hurting. I'd always been his favorite target. Now that I'd shamed myself in the eyes of Clan Campbell in full, I was more open to injury than ever before."

Thane leaned against the banister, trying to ignore the ongoing arguments about him going on in the next room. He heard Callum's voice, then others. Some positive, others aggressively inquisitive.

"At that moment," he said, continuing, "I had none of my father's rancid protection. I'd gone to the other side. I was the enemy. And Rodric was more than ready to end me slowly and painfully."

Thane blinked. The group watched him with careful eyes and fisted hands. Like they had been there with him. His heart thudded once for each of them. Despite their flaws. Despite his own blazing flaws.

"I had to completely flip what he thought I'd become."

Aini shuddered and hugged herself, but she didn't take back her demand for an answer. Thane steeled himself to continue, running a hand through his hair, then over the bump of the stone under his sweater.

"Rodric and Rabbie had a man there. A man who distributed traitorous flyers at concerts and clubs. He wasn't a true Dionadair, I don't think, but he was a rebel in his own right."

"Was he from Inverness?" Vera asked.

"Aye. They called him the Third Fiddler of Inverness."

Neve brightened. "After the old tale about the two fiddlers who spent one hundred years trapped with Thomas the Rhymer in the fairy hill?"

Thane nodded. "Most likely. This man hid flyers in a false

back of a fiddle that he played for coins. When no one was watching, he tucked statistics on the king's ordered killings in Scotland, as well as the instances of disappearances, under car windscreen wipers and into purses and through mail slots. He always disappeared before the kingsmen could get their hands on him."

Vera rubbed her hands together, obviously forgetting this tale didn't end well. "What did he look like?"

"Just an old man. Thin. Wild-eyed. He'd been handsome when he was young, probably. Had a strength to him. He fought back—"

Thane's stomach heaved and he had to stop and breathe for a moment. Aini and Bran both reached a hand out to steady him. Aini pulled her fingers back first and traded a heavy look with Myles. Thane recalled the trip home after Dodie knocked Myles out. Myles was Thane's friend now. Would he still be in five minutes? Aini wouldn't. There was no way she'd accept this. Not after how his clan had treated her father. He knew full well she could still picture Lewis's family ring on the ground and...

He had to finish the telling before he lost his nerve. He refused to lie anymore. "Rodric demanded I extract information from the fiddler. They wanted to know where the man found his information and where he hid when he wasn't on the streets. Whether the man knew more about the Dionadair than suspected. Of course, the fiddler was no coward. He clamped his mouth shut for the ones who'd taken him in and took several hard hits to the stomach and groin for his efforts."

"So they left him with you?" Vera buttoned her coat up to her chin as snow began to fall.

The icy designs drifted into Aini's hair, one thousand geometric patterns forming a crown of white.

"Aye," Thane said. "He would not break." The mask Thane

had worn his whole life, the armor of unfeeling fortitude, it slammed over Thane. It didn't fit like it used to. His heart thrummed under its weight, his new brand of thinking shining between the cracks. "I took three fingers from the man. Two from his right hand. Then one from his left before he crumbled into something far less than what he'd been."

No one said a word. The only sound was the distant rumbling of the groups inside the house and the shift of wind in the pines outside the open front door.

"Was it your tool that took the man's fingers?" Bran's voice was steady, calm.

"Ah, no. I used garden shears. Rabbie's, I suppose." Thane squeezed his fists so tightly that blood refused to flow to his knuckles and gathered painfully in his fingertips.

Bran's hand on his shoulder made him jump. "It was not your weapon. It was not your order."

"It was my choice. I could've done it another way."

"Truly?" Vera's arms fell to her sides. "Would they have taken you to Bass Rock if you'd shown anything less than total, brutal commitment to the Campbell cause?"

"No, but—"

Neve stepped closer. "You had no time. No time to make some grand plan that would save us and keep your new way of living whole. You sacrificed yourself."

"Don't call what I did heroic. I won't stand for it."

Thane's anger surged and rolled over him. It shoved him and pushed him and forced him away from the group and into the cold garden. He let the chill seep into his bones, punishing himself for the deed by imagining the fiddler's shrieks over and over and over.

CHAPTER 19
THE WEIGHT OF LOVE

A ini watched Thane walk away. Her feet wouldn't move. His hands had held her, touched her cheek, brushed her lips. And just days before, those same hands had maimed a brave, good man.

"Forgive me, Seer, but don't go thinking you're too good for him." Vera dipped her head to show some respect but her actions didn't match her tone.

"It's not that. It's just..."

Myles and Neve stood near the door, heads together, talking. He pulled her into a hug and she stayed there as he sang a silly song above her head, quiet and ridiculous and perfectly Myles.

Why couldn't her relationship be so simple?

Bran frowned at Vera. "Those sweet ones there don't carry the weight you and Thane must. You can't go around comparing yourself to them."

"I thought you didn't have a sixth sense," Aini said. "I'm pretty sure you just read my mind."

A sad smile flickered over Bran's face. "It doesn't take being a

Threader," he glanced at Vera, who was talking into her formerly hidden phone, "or a Seer to make good guesses. May I share a story with you, lass?" Bran's honest face showed the beginnings of wear, of lines around the eyes and mouth.

"Of course. And don't think I think I'm better than Thane. I just can't imagine him being the same person I spent time with right after that..."

"It's confusing. You saw Senga take a bit of control today, aye?" Aini nodded and Bran went on. "She used to do that all the time. But Nathair beat it out of her. Beat the courage out of her, both literally and figuratively. She can't handle doing the bad things it takes to fight him properly."

"She doesn't need to. We can help her."

"Exactly. Because we are now the kind that *can* do the terrible tasks a rebellion calls for." Bran leaned back a bit and studied Aini. "You'd do anything to keep your father from the king's firing squad. Wouldn't you? I can see it in you now. That ferocity. The fire and the ice. You have both. Like Thane."

"I...I don't know."

"You do. Only you aren't sitting well with it yet. Thane's had a longer journey to this spot. He knows well what it will take to defeat his father and his king. And he knows he'll get his hands dirty. He'll bend his ethics to win."

"But doesn't that make us as bad as they are? Shouldn't we stick to what we believe is right?"

Vera clenched her jaw as she studied her phone. She must've received a message from the other Dionadair. "No," she said quietly. "The win is all that matters."

Bran held up a hand. "I disagree. If we win but along the way become monsters ourselves then it's not a win, is it?"

"It's not. Not at all," Aini said. She tried to see Thane in the garden, but he'd gone past the corner and was hidden in the stone and evergreen growth. "That's what I worry about. Will this rebellion throw Thane right back into the life he fought to leave? He doesn't want to be like his father. I will not let him be like him. If that costs us the rebellion, then so be it. I will not let him become a person like Nathair Campbell or King John. There has to be another way."

"You know there isn't another way, Seer." Vera touched Aini's wrist gently. "Fate has called you both."

Aini refused to give in. Bran kept watching Aini like her face might tell him some big secret.

"What do you suggest we do when we are put in a place where winning and being a good person can't both be accomplished?" she asked.

"You must decide moment by moment," Bran said. "There is no rule or plan you can follow with this." How well this friend of Thane's already knew her. "Sometimes you'll be wrong. You'll take a false step and hurt yourself and others. But the fact that you stop and consider each move for its place on the spectrum of good and bad—that is what makes you who you are."

Myles had snuck up beside them. "You're like the old wiseman in every movie, Bran."

Bran threw a light, quick punch into Myles's stomach.

Aini's heart lifted. "You say there's no rule or plan," she said to Bran, "but that really sounded like one to me."

"If it makes you smile like that, lassie, take it for whatever you like." He hugged her, then yanked Myles and Vera into the embrace. "I love you, people. Despite your edges."

"Because of them!" Vera mumbled a shout into Aini's sleeve.

Neve jumped on top of them and let out a *Whoop!* Her mouth ended up near Aini's ear. "It's going to be all right, my friend. We're in this together. Until the end." She turned and smacked Myles's hand. "Keep your hands off until we're in private, you lout."

"I was appreciating your edges, sweetheart. My apologies." He winked at Aini, but did indeed keep his hands to himself. He was flirty, but he never seemed to press Neve into anything without her approval.

The group hug fell apart.

Vera held up her phone. "I have news. Dawn—an operative at the Glasgow main safe house—found a message from one of Nathair's code names to a kingsman that details a plan to use chemicals on the people of Edinburgh. Just as we suspected, he will blame it on the king to rouse support for himself."

"We can use this when we talk to the gathering here. I need to talk to Thane now. How long do I have?" Aini eyed the house.

"I'd say you have an hour while everyone catches up, spreads gossip, and finds something to eat," Bran said. "Then you'll both be needed inside to address the gathering formally in proper attire. There will be the fealty ceremony. After that, of course, is the dancing. Unless this goes badly."

Buzzing with fear and anticipation, Aini walked toward the garden to find Thane. She'd never thought about how fighting to be a good person made you a good person. For what felt like the thousandth time, she thanked God he'd sent Bran to Thane.

THANE TENSED WHEN SHE TOUCHED HIS ARM.

She didn't say a word. The wind blew, cold and quick, across Thane's pinked cheeks as she looked up at him. The pain on his face, in his gray eyes, tore her heart—bright, burning strips of pain across her chest. She was part of the reason he felt this way. Why had she questioned him again? Faith had to come into play here. Without it, and a heaping measure of trust, they'd never make it through the uprising.

Taking handfuls of his sweater, she pulled him close and set her forehead against his. The muscles in his arms relaxed as they slipped around her middle. His breath was soft and his skin smelled like sage and cotton. They stayed that way, a warm cocoon in the light snow shower, until a smile washed Thane's features and Aini's heart felt whole again.

Then she told Thane about Vera's news.

Thane's face was grim. "This is good. It's a stroke of good luck at last." He touched her chin. "We are going to win this thing, Aini MacGregor."

"Did you Dream it?"

"I don't need to. Reality has provided all the necessary ingredients."

"A perfect mixture for a rebellion."

"Exactly so."

IN INVERARAY CASTLE'S HIGH-CEILINGED ARMORY, AINI SAT in a red velvet chair at Thane's right hand. Vera, Myles, Neve, Bran, and Senga filled the other chairs at the head of the room. The large table had been cleared away to allow a crowd. A circle of Brown Bess rifles—all burnished steel and polished wood— made a sort of wreath over the hearth. Lochaber axes, muskets, and Scottish broadswords hung on the gold-painted walls. The tattered British flag hanging on the far wall, evidence of the Campbells long-running support of the monarchy, was disturbing to say the least. Long-handled, axe-like halberds fanned out from the rifle collection.

Aini squinted. Blood stained one of the weapons. Though

the room was cool, tension had her feeling like she was in the Grassmarket under the July sun.

Vera licked her lips in excitement. Win or lose, she was having a fine time. Aini wished she could get excited about the idea of a fight. She was ready for it, but joy was definitely not part of that.

Every time Aini glanced at Thane, he took her breath away. He'd swept his golden hair back from his face, and his gray eyes snapped clear and ready above his high cheekbones. Wearing his clan's sage green, black, and blue tartan in the old-style—hanging as a long kilt and draped over his jacket—he looked the part of a powerful chieftain.

One of Senga's men strode into the room wearing a simple black suit with a gold and black brooch in the shape of a boar's head. "The representatives are prepared to meet, Master Thane." The man bent slightly at the waist.

"Jimmy!" Thane left the table to embrace the man.

Senga smiled. "He came back as soon as he heard what was happening."

Jimmy studied Thane's face. "This is all we could ever hope for."

"Thank you for being here," Thane said. He slapped Jimmy on the back, then returned to his spot beside Aini to straighten his tartan.

This was all so formal. Aini felt completely out of place. She could almost feel every wrinkle in her new dress. Kind Senga had bought it over the phone and a girl had delivered it just fifteen minutes ago. There hadn't been time to iron the black-striped, colonial cotton skirt properly. The top was green velvet so at least no wrinkles marred that bit.

Thane stood, squaring his shoulders, and a rush of pride

soared through Aini's chest. He held a hand to her. She gripped his fingers briefly and squeezed them.

Her pulse drummed in her ears. What exactly was she going to tell these men to push them from Nathair to the Dionadair, to support Thane? Would they listen, or would they just start ripping the ancient weapons from the walls?

The thud and slap of boots carried from the dining hall and kitchens until a crowd of kilted men and finely dressed women—every age and size—had filed into the armory. Some took seats, others stood against the walls, their arms crossed over their chests.

Thane spread his arms wide. "*Fáilte*, cousins, neighbors, countrymen."

A hunched man cleared his throat loudly. He hadn't been here earlier, or at least, Aini hadn't noticed him. He squinted at Thane. "What are you planning, my lord's son?"

Another stranger, ruddy-cheeked and new to the group, pointed at Vera, Myles, and Neve. "Who are they? If you don't mind me asking."

"If you'll give me a moment, MacCoran." A muscle twitched in Thane's jaw.

Aini pulled at the high neckline of her dress. Myles winked. She gave him a weak smile. Vera bristled at the end of the row of chairs like she was ready to tackle every Campbell in the room.

Thane held up his hands. "My father, Nathair Campbell, has gone mad."

Menzies stood at the back of the room, face unreadable. Callum sat beside Senga. He rubbed his mouth with a knuckle, a mannerism Aini had noticed in Thane from time to time.

"He ravages his own countrymen—from Glasgow to Inverness to Edinburgh—for his own gain and that of the English king." Thane pounded a fist on the table and the pillar candles flamed higher. "He no longer acts like a Scotsman."

"This is foul talk, young Thane," a woman in Campbell tartan whispered. "Are you sure we just heard you right? And I want to know about what happened outside."

Callum's sharp eyes found the woman's face in the crowd. He stared. Aini wasn't sure whether he planned to shout back at her or have her shot.

But it was Menzies who spoke first. "Just listen to the man, Hawes. He...there is more happening here than you think. Believe me."

Hawes blinked, obviously surprised a man like Menzies would say something that sounded so reasonable.

Aini touched Thane's hand. *Go on. Do it.*

Senga put a hand on Thane's shoulder, tears shining in her eyes. "It's true," she said to the room. "My husband has become Scotland's worst enemy. A snake in our own grass. He is as much a monster as the false king, John III."

A man near the door threw up his hands. "Now that *is* treason!"

Others joined in, calling for Thane's arrest and spewing obscenities about the Dionadair.

But no one denied the fact that Nathair had become Scotland's worst enemy. That was something, at least. Aini's palms left marks on the table. Her heart knocked around inside her ribs.

"No." Thane's voice was thunder. "It's treason against Scotland to deny the truth. The Dionadair are our enemies no longer. To rescue our people from the machinations of my father and the false king, they follow the lead of this woman, Aini MacGregor, MacBeth's Seer."

She knew it was coming, but it didn't stop her stomach from flipping.

The room erupted into shouts and jeers.

"Criminal!"

"Take her!"

Senga, Myles, Vera, Bran, and Neve gathered around Aini and Thane. Men and women bumped against them, raising their fists. Some angled themselves toward the crowd, backing Thane and Aini.

Sweat drew down Aini's back and she reached for Thane's hand. He wrapped his long fingers around hers and held tight. She memorized the feel of the callouses and lines, and the bones of his hand and wrist.

Thane's voice stormed over the crowd. "Quiet."

"Don't you see what Nathair has become?" Aini raised her voice, making eye contact with everyone she could. "He has asked many of you to swear fealty to him alone, outside of the king and his mandates, hasn't he? Admit it."

Many looked from side to side, obviously not wanting to admit what they'd done.

"I did," one man said, raising a hand briefly. "He demanded it."

"And you think he'll do something to help us Scots? Do you truly believe he is in this to improve your life and increase your freedoms?"

"Listen to her. Do you think my father will do anything that doesn't simply feed his own power?"

"The power of the Campbells is our power too, if we support him," the man said.

Aini shook her head. "We have proof that Nathair plans to poison the people of Edinburgh."

The talking died to a murmur of questions and whispers.

"He'll put the blame on King John to gain power."

"What does he want all this power for?" a deep voice said from the back. "What claim does he have to the throne? He's not of the royal line and we'd only get more trouble from France if he wrested control away from the one who does. Am I wrong?"

There were those who spoke up in agreement and some that just put their mouths into tight lines and crossed their arms.

"Even if it did help Scotland—which most of us realize it definitely will not—is that something you can live with? Men, women, children—innocents—dead in the streets? It's horrible enough that he rips sixth-sensers and those merely accused of it from their homes."

"Where is your proof?" another voice asked. "How do we know Nathair really is ordering the city of Edinburgh poisoned?"

Callum took a slip of paper from Vera's outstretched hand and held it high. "This is the message. I believe it's valid. And I've known Nathair my whole life. You can poke holes in this all you want. But I think you know what the man is capable of."

The tension in the room weighed on Aini's shoulders. All around her, hands remained on belts where knives surely hid, sharpened and ready. One wrong move and this became a massacre with losses on all sides.

Aini cleared her throat. "When I touched the Bethune brooch, I saw the Coronation Stone." She closed her eyes and remembered she was meant to do this. "It was shaped like a seat, an ancient throne." A shiver ran up her arms. "I found MacBeth's dirk and the legendary Waymark Wall. Thane and I finally found the Coronation Stone on Bass Rock in Saint Baldred's underground cell."

Vera hefted the stone in its bag onto the table with a thud.

The gathering craned their necks to look as she pulled the burlap away to show the shining black rock.

"That's not the Coronation Stone," Hawes said. "It's too small."

But her voice trembled. They all had to feel it. The stone hummed like a beast about to spring. The gathering simply needed to see the magic for themselves.

"Thane? Shall we?" She held a hand out to him.

His smile was a sharpened blade. "Yes."

They slammed their palms onto the stone.

A roar crashed through the room, jangling the rifles against the walls and blowing the candles out. People covered their ears and cowered as the wind rushed over them, whipping around Thane and Aini, lifting their hair like flames around their heads.

Thane took their joined hands away from the ancient stone.

MacCoran grabbed his own shirt front like he was having heart trouble. Several men crossed themselves and others muttered prayers.

Thane looked ten feet tall, and Aini was pretty sure she looked just as mighty.

"Swear yourselves to your new earl," she said, "and the Heir of Scotland."

Thane's eyes found hers as he spoke to the hushed group. "We will go to Edinburgh and save the people. We will crush my father's mad quest for power. We will free Scotland from the tyranny of the English king!"

With a great shout, the representatives of the clans—kilts and skirts of peat brown, heather, blood-red, rose, midnight, and sea green—threw their fists in the air. "Aini MacGregor, our Seer, and Thane Campbell, true Heir of Scotland!"

Callum and Senga cleared everyone away.

"Back, back," Senga called out. "Time to make your allegiance official."

Jimmy and several others handed out the ceremonial swords the gathering had left on the tables. Once they had their swords on their belts, they made their mark beside their vote for Thane as chief of Clan Campbell, replacing the unfit Nathair.

MacCoran slipped out a side door. *Not today, Master MacCoran.* Aini worked through the thick of bodies and steel, following him to the corridor beyond the armory.

"Where are you going?"

The old man stopped and turned his head to glare with dark eyes. "I won't break the oath I already made to Earl Nathair. Besides, Thane cannot claim to be earl without approval from the king."

"He doesn't need the pretender's approval. He is the Heir." Vera, Neve, and Myles joined Aini. "The stone's demand overrides all," she said. "There is no shame in correcting your mistake in swearing allegiance to the wrong man."

"With all respect, I disagree." MacCoran eyed the group.

"That's fine. Vera, Neve, Myles. Would you mind helping me?"

"As you wish, Seer," Vera said before putting a gun to MacCoran's back.

"You're just going to kill me, eh? For being honorable. So glad we're gaining a new leadership. It'll be such a change."

Myles snickered. "I like him."

"We're not going to murder you, MacCoran," Aini said. "But we can't let you leave and warn our enemies of what we're up to. Vera, do you have a place you could keep him?"

"I'll think of something. Neve, give me a hand, please."

Neve jumped to open the back door and they disappeared with the man.

"That was neatly done," Myles said. "Now, I think it's time for a bunch of Scots to promise their souls to you and Thane or something."

"I don't think souls will be mentioned. Just defense."

"Tomato, tomatooooeeee." Myles held out a hand toward the armory and nodded for her to go in first.

"Thanks." She grinned.

"Of course, my liege."

"Please stop."

"I don't think so. This is the fun part."

Incorrigible.

CHAPTER 20
BE IT KENNED TO ALL

One by one, each clan representative and their associates lined up in front of Thane and Aini.

Callum was the first.

His wiry, gold-red hair swept away from his wide face, he went down on one knee and set his sword on the ground. Holding his palms up, he spoke low, but loud enough that most could hear.

"Be it kenned to all, I bind and oblige my heirs and myself by the faith and truth in my body to maintain, assist, defend, and concur with Thane Campbell, Earl of Argyll and Chief of Clan Campbell and his heirs and sundries their quarrels, actions, debates, and causes from this date."

Thane took Callum's hand in both of his. He nodded his head, then looked to Aini. Callum inclined his head to her. He put a hand over his heart.

"I give my respect to you, Seer. I'm amazed this old man has the chance to see this prophecy come to fruition."

Aini copied the gesture and rested her fingers over the soft, velvet neckline of her dress. Her heart beat, sure and steady, under her palm. "I promise to do my best to fulfill the role Fate has given to me."

One by one, the rest came forward and bent the knee to them.

Thane wasn't wearing a crown, but he sure did look like a king with the sun streaming through the windows and touching his head, and the crowd in quiet reverence as they listened to his responses. Aini never would've said it aloud—too crass, and it wasn't important right now—but that look of power and capability was very, very attractive.

When the ceremony finished, Myles and Neve found Aini and handed her a glass of wonderfully cold ice water. She drank it down and felt more hopeful than she had in days.

"The real question of the day is, what the heck does *kenned* mean?" Myles took the glass and ate one of Aini's ice pieces.

"Known," Neve said. "Let it be known."

Myles gave her a nod. "All right. I'm satisfied. Now, when does this dancing they've been bragging about start up? Let it be kenned I'm ready to set the floor on fire." He shimmied against Neve's hip and she bumped him, grinning.

The twang and pluck of musicians readying their instruments trickled from the saloon.

"I'm guessing now?" Aini led them to the saloon's door. "I'm going to freshen up a little. I'll meet you in a minute or two."

They took off to mingle with those already gathered on the pale wood floors as Aini escaped to the restroom to have some much needed quiet.

A HALF HOUR LATER, VIOLINS AND DRUMS FOUGHT FOR attention in the long, wide expanse of the saloon. Everyone was dancing the same reel, but it looked like poorly managed chaos to Aini.

"Good evening, lovely," Thane said from behind her making her jump. His warm hands circled her waist and the length of him pressed against her gently. "Are we going to dance or stand here plotting?"

"There is a lot of planning to do." Weapons. Locations. Information. Father had sent coded intel from Edinburgh an hour ago regarding Lord Darnwell—the French queen's brother-in-law—as well as kingsmen movements near Edinburgh. The rebels had a true army to assemble. And Nathair was still "off the map" as Menzies had put it. Disconcerting, to say the least.

"I know planning *is* your favorite past time, but could you spare a few minutes for me?" Thane's breath on her neck turned her insides to molten silver.

"I think I can do that."

She led him into the reel, her body finding the music and settling into its rhythm. His grin lit her up as she spun, then returned to his hands.

"Are you wearing the stone?" she asked. The leather strap wasn't showing on his neck.

He tapped the tooled, black leather bag attached to one of two belts on his kilt. "It's safe in my sporran." With a wink, he started dancing again.

The room was hot, but it wasn't unpleasant. A ton of candles scented the air with beeswax and brightened the wood-framed portraits of Thane's fancy ancestors. Vera and Bran argued beside the perspiring musicians.

Thane nodded toward them as he took Aini's hand and moved right two steps. "Should we intervene?"

"They're just two very different people," Aini said. "Hopefully their shared interest in this rebellion will bridge the distance."

"Like the recent study that showed how agrin and acetylcholine surprisingly work together to develop our synaptic connections..." Thane trailed off as Aini gave him a look. "You know," he said, sounding casual which only made Aini want to laugh and punch him a little, "like our muscle cells and motor neurons and all that."

"All that. Yeah."

"I'm not the only nerd here, Organization Queen."

She patted his back. "Truth." They moved away from the dancing and toward the armory.

Menzies stood talking to Senga. All the faces that had stood out in the fighting and arguing were here except maybe Callum. He was probably off doing some of that organization she should've been overseeing.

Aini drank in the sight of Thane walking in front of her. The flash of his leg and boot below the edge of his kilt. The broad lines of his back. The quick, mischievous smile he threw her over his muscled shoulder.

Yeah. She could wait on the organization for an hour or three.

Candles in the room where they'd shown off the larger chunk of the Coronation Stone flickered in sconces beside the arrays of swords and axes.

"Will you come up to my rooms with me?" Thane asked, his voice a little rough.

A thrill went through Aini. "Yes."

A stairwell hid behind the armory. Aini let Thane lead her further from the noise of the celebrating. The stairs brought them to a small room papered in silken black and green stripes.

A massive four poster bed boasted a Campbell tartan canopy and a twisted, dark wood frame.

"Is this really your room?" Sometimes Aini forgot how Thane had grown up. Then she saw things like this. "This bed could eat mine."

A spark lit his eyes. "It's nice to have plenty of room."

Aini's mouth dropped open and her knees were suddenly about as sturdy as a bowl of pudding.

He held out a hand. "Did I say the wrong thing?" He looked genuinely worried.

"No. No." She cleared her throat and put a hand on one of her burning cheeks. "I just wasn't expecting that." She laughed, enjoying the fact that everyone else was very, very far away.

As he stood there, looking delicious, Aini gave up any thought of clever talk.

She pretty much attacked him.

They fell onto the bed and Aini froze for a second, her chest on his. She reached out and brushed a fingertip over his eyebrow, then down his temple where his pulse tapped quickly. Something was pressing into her.

"Ah," he whispered, wiggling hands beneath her and making her gasp. "It's my sporran." He pulled off the small bag and threw it to the floor.

"Might want to be a little more careful with that, seeing as your most powerful weapon is sitting inside."

His gaze flamed hot across her body. "I have other weapons, hen."

Aini swallowed. His hair was wild. She realized she was straddling him with very little clothing separating them. She met his eyes and saw what she needed to see—permission to keep up her attack.

Her mouth found his jawline. The soft stubble on his skin

pricked her lips lightly. His large hands smoothed their way down her back, then drifted over her hips before latching on with a strong grip that made her head swim wonderfully. She started unbuttoning his shirt, taking moments here and there to run fingers over his warm skin. He made a growling sort of noise, and before she knew it, she was on her back, his hips pinning her down delightfully. He raised himself up and looked down. One of her legs was between his, the kilt swinging and tickling her leg through her stockings.

She reached forward and set a hand on his thigh, daring herself to go further. His chest rose and fell like he'd sprinted miles after eating altered caramels. He seemed barely able to hold himself still. His fingers shook, and she couldn't help but love that she had that effect on him. The candles along the wall flickered and snapped, sending shadows across the striped silk walls.

Thane put his hand over hers and scooted her fingers a little higher. Raising an eyebrow, he grinned wickedly. "Go on then, aye. If you want..."

Then a knife appeared at Thane's throat.

CHAPTER 21
BOOM

The staccato of gunfire broke across the house, shattering a window not far from the saloon. Bran slowly set his whisky glass on the table as men and women shouted and went for weapons hidden inside their fine clothes. Senga hurried in from the hallway beyond. A piece of her silver hair had broken free and curved under her chin.

"It's Nathair's men," she said to him. "I know it."

"How?" Bran joined her at the saloon's door as another volley of shots pounded the stone walls outside. "Why aren't they coming in? What do they want?"

"It's him. And a small group he recently brought together for the jobs that matter most, he says. A new group of sycophants he picked up in the roughest parts of Glasgow and Birmingham. They're petty gang thugs who think they'll get the best spots when he pushes the king from Scotland. They aren't loyal to any clan. Only to him. They're outside our politics, really, and I have no idea what he's ordered them to accomplish here now."

"He could've been in here with all of us dead by now considering he wiggled past the guard already without us knowing." It didn't make any sense.

"Aye." Senga's gaze tore across the room. "Where is my son?"

"With Aini. Upstairs." Bran gave Senga a knowing look and she almost smiled, but she knew as well as Bran that they were in serious danger.

Vera, a few of her rebels, and two of Callum's men spoke together in a corner. Vera was pointing toward the back of the house.

"I'll see what I can do to find Thane and Aini. To secure them," Bran said to Senga.

"I'll arm everyone here." Senga slipped back out of the room with her trusted butler in tow.

"Vera," Bran called. She looked up at him, eyes wild. Neve and Myles gathered beside them. "We need to find Thane and Aini."

"Mac," she called to a man turning tables over to block the entrance. The man hurried over and she spoke quickly in his ear. With a nod, he ran off.

Bran wanted more than anything to go warn his best mate himself, but he had other duties at the moment. At least Thane and Aini were in an interior room. "I have three explosive devices armed and ready in the back of the truck out there," Bran said. "Right beside their gunners."

"What are they doing? It's Nathair, isn't it?" Neve turned toward the door.

"Senga thinks so," Bran said, stomach clenching with dread. "Whoever it is, they deserve some boom, I'd say."

"Agreed." Myles nodded and squeezed his hands into fists at his sides.

Senga returned and began handing out revolvers and rifles and night sticks.

"When do you think I should put them off—" Bran's question was cut by a loud crash coming from the front steps and a rain of bullets into what sounded like the upper story windows.

"Now is good, right? How about now?" Myles grimaced.

Bran pulled three tiny switch boxes from his interior jacket pocket. "Sounds good to me." They'd have to time this right though. They couldn't hit their own people and they had to take down as many of Nathair's group as possible. "I'm going to need some eyes on the scene out there."

They followed him through the house and into the dining room beside the front entrance hall.

"Don't turn the lights on," Bran said to Myles who had a hand on the dial.

Myles slowly removed his fingers from the light switch.

Shapes moved in the moonlight outside a broken window. A man shouted at the house, but his words were drowned by his own handgun firing, bright white in the near darkness.

"They're not close enough to the truck," Bran said.

"But you have three high explosives?" Vera pulled the curtain aside a fraction and peered south. "How strong?"

"They'll blow the back of the truck apart and take anyone within, say, ten feet."

"I have this," Neve said, holding up one of those caramels Thane had made. "I...I can eat one. Maybe run out there and draw them toward the truck?"

"Nope." Myles crossed his arms and shook his head.

"I appreciate your courage, Neve," Vera said, "but we don't need a suicide mission on this. Ideas, Bran?"

Bran pursed his lips, thinking. "Maybe if they believe we need something in there, they'll investigate it. Do you have a walkie?"

Vera handed him one of the small ones the Dionadair always

used. If he spoke into it in a place Nathair's men would overhear him, if he handled it right, he might push them into checking the truck out, then *kaboom*, and hopefully Thane would escape what Bran feared would be his end.

In the room opposite this one, wind blew the fine, black curtains, fluttering them like giant corbie wings. "Has your Mac sent word back about Thane and Aini?" Bran asked.

"No." She followed him to the room across the hall, Myles and Neve on her heels.

Bran held the walkie to his mouth to begin his acting. It took nothing to make his voice sound strained. "It's in the truck. We have to get in there before they do. We can't move forward without it."

There was no guarantee the men outside the broken window would hear him and take the bait. He could hear feet on the drive and the occasional shout of orders to move. Another walkie talkie was loud with white noise, but Bran couldn't catch any snippets of conversation. There was too much other racket.

"Yes," Bran said into the walkie, louder now. "We need inside the Dionadair truck. Now."

Vera gasped. She knew as well as he did that mentioning the presence of the rebels would end any chance they might still have had for surprise.

He gripped Vera's arm.

Myles and Neve cocked guns and held them ready for anyone who might come through the door.

"I think they're here for Thane and Aini," Bran said, realizing this was the truth and that he'd really known it from the first moment.

Vera pulled away and flew out of the room, obviously heading for Thane and Aini and those she'd sent after them. "Mac! Greta!"

Outside, three men crept toward the truck. It wasn't all of them, but it was better than none.

Bran flipped all three switches. Three red lights bloomed in his hands. "Myles. Neve." He gave each of them a detonator, keeping an eye on Nathair's men. One man threw the back of the truck open. "Hit the button exactly when I hit mine. All right?" They nodded. "Now."

All three pressed their detonators, and with a blast to make ears ring, the night was day for a few seconds of horror. The truck belched flame and smoke as it leaped from the drive. The explosion sent all three of Nathair's men into the grass where they lay knocked clean out. They were lucky they weren't dead. An engine revved in the muffled aftershock of noise in Bran's ears.

Someone was leaving.

He tore out of the room, beelining for Thane's bedroom. Why hadn't he gone himself when he'd first heard the shots?

If Nathair had done what Bran feared, Bran would never, ever forgive himself for this mistake. Palms soaked, heart driving into his mouth, praying, praying, praying, he raced past the Dionadair, Campbells, and Gowries and into the darkness of Inveraray's secret passages.

CHAPTER 22
DEADLY DREAMS

From Heaven to Hell. In a blink.

Cold metal bit into Thane's throat and he heard his father's rasping voice at his ear. "Stop rutting and listen to me, just for a moment?"

Thane silently berated himself. Why had he thrown his sporran to the floor? "How did you find me, Nathair?"

"This is my house, boy."

Aini's face paled. She tugged her skirt down. Thane stepped off the bed and marched backward, the edge of the knife pushing him. He was dizzy and couldn't seem to get his feet under him properly.

"We have an army here," Aini snapped, hair over one side of her face and cheeks bright pink. "Even if you kill both of us, you'll never get out of here alive." She eyed the door, probably wondering what was happening in the saloon right now.

Nathair stopped. "That army down there is mine, you traitorous witch."

Thane turned and took the sting of the knife.

"Aye," Nathair hissed. "I do know what she is. And you too. Dreamer. Seer." He snorted and let the knife release a stream of hot blood down Thane's neck.

Thane felt no pain. Only panic. His heart was in his mouth because Aini was here and so was this beast of a man who'd killed so many like her so many times in so many ways.

"It is a bit of a mess though. I'll give you that, my son." He said the last word like it put the taste of poison on his tongue.

Then Thane's most recent Dream flooded his mind. The mountain of loose rock and how his foot slipped, the faraway ground looming, shimmering, dizzying. He saw again Aini's blood red dress and heard the old king Kenneth MacAlpin's words.

Choose. We will see what kind of king you'll be.

This was the choice.

Would he fall like he had in the Dream? His throat tightened and bobbed against the sharp metal edge of his father's weapon.

"If you let her go, if you leave those downstairs alone, I'll go with you willingly."

He could almost see Aini's face dissolving as he fell away, off the mountain in his Dream.

Her eyes blazed. "You're not doing this, Thane."

"What makes you think I'd do that?" Nathair asked.

"Because," Thane said, "Rodric told me you wanted a show. And you could put on such a great one with me as Heir and Dreamer and asking for mercy at your feet."

This was the only way Aini and the others might just have a chance to escape with their lives.

Aini's fists loosened and she held out a hand, tears shining on her cheeks. "I won't just go. Not without you."

"You will."

"You'll do exactly as I say, lass." Nathair put the knife against

Thane's ear and drew a line of lancing pain from lobe to temple. "If you want this fool to live."

"You're the fool," she said to Nathair.

"Aini, please." Thane would beg. He would do anything to get her out of this room. "Just go. Stay quiet. It'll be all right. I love you, hen. I do. And this is the only way I save you. It's too late for me. I should've known. I am a Campbell and I'll always be trapped by my family name." Tears burned the edges of his eyes. He'd never see her again after this. Or if he did, he'd be under Nathair's control and he'd be her enemy. "Please just flee Scotland. Go back to the colonies. Anywhere. This rebellion was doomed from the start." He had actually believed they'd be successful. Why did he keep tricking himself? His father was right. He was a fool.

She snorted and crossed her shaking arms. "I'm not going along with this, Nathair. Absolutely not. You'll kill us regardless so I might as well make life difficult for you." She locked eyes with Thane. What was she doing?

She opened her mouth and screamed.

The door swung open. Callum walked in and Aini's mouth clamped shut. Thane sighed. They were saved.

Callum lowered a hunting rifle at Aini.

Thane frowned. What was the man doing?

The initials CG were etched into Callum's gun barrel, elegant and proud. "Shut it, lassie," Callum said, "before things grow far worse than you ever could've imagined."

But Callum was on their side. "Uncle? What is this?"

Aini's face showed a war between confusion and rage as she took a step back.

Callum kept his gaze on her, but spoke to Thane. "I wanted to support you, young Thane. I wasn't lying to you."

No. NO. This could not be happening.

"But your father has a way of persuading people to do what he needs them to do."

Thane's anger was a fist around his chest, keeping him from taking a breath. "Father. What did you do?"

"Callum is a good man," Nathair said. "He is most concerned about the well-being of the people of Perthshire. I simply let him know that it wouldn't go well with them if he made a wrong choice in this little...disturbance."

"This is a rebellion." Aini was the embodiment of righteous anger.

Thane regarded Callum like he was some strange creature he'd never seen. "So you told him where I would be. You set up the empty hallway. Did you kill the guards we had set on the stairs?"

A flicker of unease crossed Callum's face. "No. I gave them a chore and it was all very peaceful. I'm not the enemy here."

Aini stepped closer to the gun and made Thane's legs go limp. Nathair caught him under the arm roughly.

"You're the worst kind of enemy," she said. "You betrayed us!"

"My people are my only family now." Grief gave Callum's words weight. Thane was forced to believe his uncle truly hadn't wanted to do this, to report Thane's whereabouts to Nathair and make this turn possible. The fact just made Thane's hatred of his father grow deeper, darker.

"I don't think she's going to let you make this choice, son," Nathair said.

She had to. "Aini, please." He poured all his love into his pleading. "Go. I can't stand the thought that the world wouldn't have you anymore. I can't..." Tears broke free of his eyes and joined the warm blood on his throat. He didn't care that his nightmare of a father was listening and sneering. This was about Aini's life. The life of the woman who shoved the heavy cloak of evil away to see the good hiding deep inside Thane's shattered soul. "If you live on, the best part of me will too."

A sob choked Aini. She drew a hand across her cheek.

Callum kept the gun on her, but his face had gone white.

"Enough." Nathair dragged Thane out the door. "You make sure she stays quiet until we're gone and I'll keep to my end of the bargain, Callum."

Callum nodded once, then lifted a boot to shut the door between them.

The last thing Thane saw was Aini's face glistening with tears, and panic in her eyes. Then Nathair struck him hard on the temple and he knew no more.

THANE WOKE UP IN THE BACK OF TRUCK, HIS HANDS AND FEET bound with twine and attached to the wall via a zip tie. Looking through the window between the cargo hold and the cab, he could see Nathair's sharp profile in the driver's seat. The events in his room at Inveraray hadn't been a mere nightmare. All of it had actually happened.

The stone.

Thane scanned the floor, longing to see the sporran that held the stone necklace but also praying it was far, far away from Nathair. There. In the back corner—barely visible because of both the lack of light and the absence of Thane's glasses—sat his sporran and the larger chunk of the Coronation Stone in its burlap bag. Nathair had secured both. All Thane needed to fight off Nathair was right there. So close, but completely out of reach. Thane knew his father well enough to realize Nathair had arranged this situation to further deflate any hope Thane might have. Thane shut his eyes and leaned his head against the vibrating truck bed.

He would never see Aini again.

His cruel mind brought forward an image of her laugh, the dimple in her cheek, the sound of his name on her tongue. Then he saw Callum's gun and imagined a gun shot and could almost see her falling, bloodstained and broken, to the floor at his traitor uncle's boots.

Thane was turned inside out, emptied.

The truck bumped down some unknown road, and his head rapped sharply on the metal grating, reminding him that his father had nearly cut his ear off. But Thane didn't move to relieve the pain. He pressed into it, relishing the way it burned the imaginations away.

What would happen to the rebellion now that they had no Heir? He prayed with all his might that they would go on without him and defeat the king and bring someone else to power. At the same time, he begged God to get Aini out of the country before any more harm came to her. Maybe wise Bran could talk her into leaving.

Bran. Thane wouldn't see him again either, he supposed. Bran had been the brother Thane always wanted. What would Bran do now? He was caught between two worlds—the Dionadair and the Campbells. No matter what Bran did, someone would want him dead.

Thane couldn't stand the fact that he wouldn't be able to communicate with any of them, to see what was going on and if they'd escaped Nathair this time. They could all be dead right now. Aini, Myles, Neve, Bran, Vera. Senga.

Mother.

Thane swallowed bile. "Did you see mum?" he shouted toward the glass dividing him from Nathair.

"What's that?" Nathair barked back as he buzzed the window down.

"I said, did you see my mother?"

"She surprised me. I had no idea she could stir up so much trouble. She's been dealt with. Now it's best if you remain ignorant on the details. Be a good lad and keep your end of the bargain or I'll find that girl of yours and she won't like what happens then." He raised the window back up and the truck lunged, increasing in speed.

Thane fought the urge to vomit. He was lying. Mother was fine. She had to be fine. If she wasn't...

He could almost smell her perfume and hear her singing at the well where she used to take him on Sundays.

CHAPTER 23
IN THE DARKNESS

The door swung shut. Aini's arms wouldn't move to tear Callum's rifle from his hands. Her feet were stuck to the dark carpeting of Thane's bedroom and a pathetic fluttering between her ribs said there used to be a functioning heart somewhere inside her. She couldn't let this happen.

Move, she demanded her body. *Do something.*

With Callum's side to her, his gaze not directly aimed her way, she jammed her shoe into the back of his knee. He exhaled in a great huff and nearly toppled over.

"Stop that." The gun barrel lifted, level to her nose. "I don't want to hurt you, so stay still, lass. Just for a few more minutes. Then it'll all be over."

"It won't be over. You gave Thane to Nathair and I will never, ever stop fighting to free him."

Callum studied the ceiling and sighed heavily. "Then you'll die and your friends with you."

"We are prepared for that."

"Are you? Do you even know what it feels like to lose someone you love, you, just a slip of a girl?"

A memory of her mother's hands flashed through her mind. Delicate. Strong. Music made flesh. "I know exactly how that feels." But she wasn't about to share the loss of her mother with this betraying arse. "Didn't you learn anything from Lady Greensleeves?"

Callum's face went red with rage. "I did. I made my apologies. This is nothing like that. I'm actually saving your life. If you rebel now, I will simply act as ordered by the one I swore fealty to. The first one. My men know nothing of this yet, but I will explain it all and they will understand. Everyone downstairs will. Maybe even you. I'm only protecting us from Nathair's rage. He is the man we must follow or we'll all suffer. I'm protecting you, my people, and those loyal to Clan Campbell. There's no shame in that."

"Isn't there?"

"I'm protecting my people. And following the king's law."

"King John isn't supposed to be king. Don't you get it? The prophecy and the stone named Thane as the Heir. John is a pretender, a monster, a fraud we must rise up against. You don't think someday Nathair and John will come for you again? You don't think they'll ask something horrible from you and your people? You truly believe they'll leave your little bubble in Perth happy and free? And even if Nathair does for some wild reason keep his word and protect your people, he is rising against the king himself. The king will come for you. Do you truly believe you'll make it out of this mess without a scratch just by playing the role of submissive subject?" She let out a Vera-like laugh. "You're an idiot. Thane gave you far, far too much credit."

The sound of his name made her stomach tighten. Had they already left the grounds and escaped? Were Nathair's men murdering and maiming everyone downstairs? She tried to look out the window, but Callum knocked the gun into her shoulder. He started to say something, but she cut him off.

"He loved you." She stared into his bulbous eyes, forcing him to see the truth. "And you betrayed him. Do you know how many people Thane trusts? How many he loves like family?"

Callum blinked. "His mother stands with him and I'll see she is cared for."

"She doesn't want to be cared for. She wants to be able to trust a man who called himself her brother-in-law and in heart to keep his promises. Senga is a rebel who refuses to live in a bubble and ignore the rest of the country's needs!"

There was a shout outside the door, then the ground shook. The glass in the window buzzed. Callum let the gun fall, and Aini launched herself into him, knocking him to the ground. Untangling herself, she kicked him in the nose and jerked the door open.

Bran was on the stairs, fear written all over his face. "Where is Thane?"

Aini tried to say the words *He is gone*, but they wouldn't come. Her throat was thick and her tongue stuck to the roof of her mouth.

Bran took a labored breath. "That's what I was afraid of. It was Nathair himself, wasn't it?"

Aini nodded, then started quickly down the steps, going past him. "Callum is back there with a broken nose to match his broken promise."

"Really?" Bran's footsteps were close behind. "He ratted Thane out?"

"I don't think he planned on doing it, but yes. Nathair threatened Perth as a whole and Callum folded under the weight of immediate danger rather than using his good head to realize we're all trapped and starving with the government the way it is right now."

"You sound like a real Dionadair," Vera said as she appeared from the armory to meet them. "Bran. Nice explosion."

"Thane is gone," Bran said, sparing Aini from having to say the words aloud. "Nathair has him."

"Did Nathair sic his men on you?" Aini's stomach clenched and rolled over. She gripped Vera and Bran. "I need...I need a second." She bent and let her head hang between her knees until the nausea faded. "Okay. I'm all right. Tell me. What's going on?"

Bran held up a hand. "Mac is injured, right?" he asked Vera.

"Aye, but I can send someone else to deal with Callum."

"We need to keep Callum here. And quiet," Aini said. "His men don't know—and they can't be allowed to find out—that he betrayed us. It'll only weaken us. Do you think you can change his mind about us, Bran? Get him to support Thane and me?"

"Maybe. Doubt it. But I know a secret passageway from Thane's room. Vera, can you get two of yours to take him under the house? If you get Senga's butler to help them, he can show you where to hide Callum until we know what to do with him. They can take Nathair's men injured from the blast too."

As Vera spoke into a phone, she led them through the armory. After giving her orders, she turned to Aini. "Nathair only brought a small contingent of armed men. They were obviously here as a distraction, so Bran gave them something to deal with. We figured you and Thane had some trouble coming at you."

"You were right." The blades on the walls seemed to stare down at them, silver, steely eyes. "We should use these weapons. They're antiques, right? If Senga thinks it's a good idea, we should carry them and tell everyone we have them and use them to show the clan representatives that we can return to the glory days when Scotland was a power on its own and France was its ally against England."

Bran was nodding. "Aye. Not many here have family fighting the French. Not yet anyway. If we can angle things so that they see France as a potential ally against King John—"

"You mean the false king John," Vera said.

"Exactly that," Bran said. "Then they may see this rebellion as having a better chance of ending in success and peace."

"Even with the Heir in Nathair's hands?" Vera stopped, and Aini nearly ran her over. "Wait. Did he take the stone necklace, Aini?"

"He did. But we have the larger piece still, don't we?"

"No. Nathair's men mowed our four guards down and nabbed it from Senga's room."

"She is okay though?" Aini asked.

"She is, but when she learns her greatest fear has come true..." Bran traded a look with Aini.

"I'll go to her." She didn't want to be the one to give Senga the news, but it felt right somehow. Thane would want Aini to tell her. "Where is she?"

"In the library, looking for a coded letter Nathair wrote to the French years ago. She thinks it might help drive a wedge between him and the false king," Vera said.

"I'll go there now. I'll meet you both in the armory with anyone who wants to discuss strategy in one hour."

Because of what she'd gone through with her father, Aini knew fear for Thane would come again and freeze her where she stood. She had to get as much accomplished as possible before she was locked in the ice, worrying about a loved one trapped in the hands of an enemy.

SENGA'S HANDS MOVED QUICKLY THROUGH A STACK OF PAPER on a huge, mahogany desk in the corner of the library. Books lined the walls and soaked in the sound of Aini's footsteps.

Senga must've heard her anyway. Her head lifted and she set those gray eyes, so much like Thane's, on Aini. Her fingers released the papers and fanned over the stack. "Where is Thane?"

Aini cleared her throat and pushed the words out of her reluctant mouth. "Nathair took him at knifepoint. He wants to use him in a display of sorts to quell this rebellion."

Senga's hand went to a knife tucked into her belt. "We will find him and free him."

"Nathair doesn't have a chance."

Senga smiled as tears welled around her pale eyelashes. She held out her hands and Aini squeezed them. The fear Aini had been holding back stole over her with a corpse-like chill. Her teeth chattered.

"Here," Senga said. "Sit." She motioned toward the desk chair.

Aini had tried to act like they would be able to rescue Thane and tried to believe it herself. But it was impossible. Nathair would never leave his side again. He'd have a true army surrounding him. Even if they could charge at Nathair, Aini had no doubt Nathair would shoot Thane down before he let him escape. Thane was as good as dead.

"It'll be all right," Senga whispered, turning to pick up a fuzzy, tartan blanket. Tucking it around Aini and settling her into the chair, she knelt. "We will make a plan. That'll make you feel better."

Aini should've been doing this for her, not the other way around. "I'm sorry. I'm fine. You're right." She reached for a tissue on the desk and wiped her nose. Her hands shook so hard she dropped the tissue, and Senga retrieved it.

"I'll get you some tea." Senga stood and hurried out of the room, head held high.

Would she give in to her fear in the kitchens, away from Aini?

Aini hated herself. She had to be strong, but all she could see behind her closed eyes was blood running down Thane's throat and the terror in his eyes. The finality in that look he gave her— that was the thing that stopped the blood in her veins and dissolved her hope that he'd fight his way out of Nathair's hands or someone was coming to help. That look had said goodbye as loudly as the slam of the door.

Tugging the blanket more tightly around her, Aini covered her face and recalled every moment with Thane. She had to burn the images into her head so she wouldn't lose them. It was all she had left now. It would have to be enough to get her through this rebellion.

Should they even go on with the rebellion? What was the point now? There was no Heir. No ghost kings to fight John. Callum had left their side. The Dionadair would lose. They would all rot in prison or fall to the firing squad's bullets.

"Thane," Aini whispered into the blanket. "I hope you know I loved you."

She imagined his tortured look, the goodness all tied up in the pain. She could almost feel his hands cupping her face and the brush of his mouth on hers. He'd battled such terrible darkness to become a man she could be with. Gone against his own father. Fought for hers. He'd tortured that poor rebel for her father and for her. He'd given up his very soul to protect Aini, her father, Myles, Neve, and Senga. He'd done horrible things to keep them alive.

"I will never forget what you did for us."

The bruised light streaming through the curtains slid over her hands, shadowing them and making her bones stand out like she was a corpse herself. A part of her had certainly died and there was no way to bring it back to life. The words came at last and brought with them a finality nothing else could. Her skeleton trembled under her skin as she spoke quietly to the dust motes floating around her face.

"Thane. Is. Gone."

THE LIBRARY DOOR OPENED AND SENGA CAME IN WITH A TEA tray. Myles and Neve trailed her. Myles was straight-faced. Neve's eyes were too wide and she clenched and unclenched fists at her sides.

Senga set the tea on the table and began pouring out the amber liquid. Steam rose to join the dust in the purple light. Aini wanted to throw off her blanket, serve the tea herself, and demand Senga take some time to mourn the day's events, but grief held her in unmovable claws.

Myles sat on the desk in front of Aini, then decided to lie down, asking Senga permission with a look. Neve sat on the arm of the chair and set her chin on Aini's head. They didn't say anything, but their simple presence stopped Aini's shivering.

She shut her eyes and leaned into Neve, letting the world crash around her.

CHAPTER 24
A BROTHER LOST

Bran fell against the garden wall, his back hitting the hard surface and knocking what little breath he had out of him.

He hadn't wanted to break open in front of Aini or Senga. Lord knew they didn't need further evidence that Thane in Nathair's hands was the worst of nightmares. A chill rushed over Bran's flesh and he closed his eyes.

Nathair would know exactly how to hurt Thane. He'd have someone beat him, of course, as punishment for being a traitor, but that wouldn't be the worst of it. The mind games would be darkest part of Thane's time with him. He'd twist every deed Thane had done and peel it apart to somehow make it seem like Thane was the reason for every problem in the world.

And that promise the foolish lad had believed about Nathair leaving Aini alone? It was only a matter of time before Nathair launched some plan to get her as well. Bran wasn't sure why he hadn't already taken her. It wasn't easy untangling a man's mind. Not an evil genius's mind like Nathair's. Bran would bet all that it was meant to create the utmost torture for Thane and the best angle for Nathair's play for power in Scotland.

Maybe he'd use Thane against the king. Or hand Thane to the king to soften the king toward Nathair. There were a million possibilities and every one of them ended with Bran's best mate, his chosen brother, in terrible pain, and after that, most likely dead.

Bran kicked the wall with a heel and let out a curse, sending a flock of black birds into the lead sky. Without the Heir, without the stone, where did they all stand? Was there any chance here to turn this around?

He thought of Aini's fierce eyes, her tears only making her passion all the more genuine. Aini. The Seer. She was what they had, and she might be enough. She had to be enough.

Bran pushed off the wall and stared toward Edinburgh. He would stand with his best mate's girl and together with the rebels; they would at the very least give that evil genius some real trouble. He headed toward the Dionadair crowding the drive.

"Who has Macbeth's knife?" he demanded, hope surging inside his aching chest.

A woman raised a hand. "I do. Been keeping it safe on Vera's orders."

"Then come with me, please." He started toward the door. "Our Seer needs us now more than ever."

The vibes of the group behind him gave him the strength to open the door and begin the next grueling step in this revolution.

CHAPTER 25
THE STEEL TO RISE

Minutes, hours, days, an eternity later, the door opened and one of the older men from the safe house back in Greenock strode up to the desk.

"Vera just spoke to a Ms. Smith, of the Magnolia Plantation in the southern colonies. She claims to have wired a very large sum of money to a coded account for Myles and what she called his *difficulties*."

Myles popped up. "Since when does she care?"

The messenger nodded. "Ms. Smith declared that no one is permitted to treat her son poorly. That she will not allow it."

Myles threw up his hands. "Yeah. Only she can treat me like crap. Tell her she can shove her money. I refuse to take it."

"But Mr. Smith..."

"It would be useful, Myles," Neve said.

"I can't." Myles sat back down. "I just can't let her be a part of my life. Not anymore."

Aini touched his shoulder and nodded.

The messenger looked to each of them, then seemed

resigned to Myles's decision. "Fine then. I will inform those involved. The money will be not be used."

"I wonder what she'll make of that," Myles said. "I've never turned money down."

Neve kissed his temple.

Bran walked in. What appeared to be the entirety of the gathering of clans and Dionadair behind him. They filed in and stood silent.

Aini studied the gathering and swallowed.

"We come to honor you, support you, and arm you, Seer," Bran said, rather formally.

A woman stepped forward and placed a familiar knife in Aini's hands. Bog oak hilt. The scent of history and power clouding around its ancient fittings and blade.

Her hand clasped it with a mind of its own and strength flowed through her like a shot of adrenaline. She tucked it firmly into her waistband and raised her eyes to the group, her pulse steady and loud in her ears.

"I won't go over what we already know. What you may not know is that I am never going to give up on Thane or this rebellion. Not until my hearts stops beating. And if you're with me, I say we put our heads together and make a plan to liberate our Heir!"

Vera crossed her thumbs and shouted, the room joining in. Myles, Neve, Bran, and Senga stood by Aini's sides, determination sharpening their features.

She turned away from the group to stare into the starlit sky. Her heart thudded in her throat, pushing her blood through her body so quickly she felt like she was falling. Her mind showed her images of every vision she'd ever had.

Mother in a wedding gown.

Father holding her as a baby.

Thane in the garden with Senga and Nathair.

Myles's mother.

Ghosts and memories, emotions like a whirlwind of color nearly overwhelmed her. She put a hand to the cold, cold window and spoke like Thane still stood next to her, powerful and prepared.

"We will rise, Thane. We are coming for you. Never forget who you are."

Read the conclusion of Aini and Thane's story in The Edinburgh Fate!

*Please consider leaving a review for The Edinburgh Heir.
Reviews are important for readers like you!*

If you'd like to sign up for Alisha's mailing list and receive two complementary prequels to this series and an epic fantasy series as well, check out alishaklapheke.com.

Now, continue on for a sneak peek at Alisha's high fantasy, Waters of Salt and Sin, perfect for fans of Sabaa Tahir, Sarah J Maas, and Kristin Cashore!

After the chapter, enjoy a fun Scots slang dictionary!

SAMPLE: WATERS OF SALT AND SIN

Chapter One

A BREATH BEFORE SUNRISE, THE SEA WAS A HALF-LIDDED EYE, pale blue and white beyond the town walls and lemon orchards. The sea and me, the only two awake this early. Or so it seemed when I climbed to the roof of the tavern. The streets were only dark mud and shuttered windows. I should've been scouring, looking for a fallen dumpling or a bit of orange-spiced chicken. But I couldn't help myself. The glimmering saltwater winked at me and I gave it a lazy smile.

"Soon," I whispered before heading back down.

I had to finish the rope I'd labored on all night, because though magic was good for a lot of things, unfortunately, twisting coconut fibers wasn't one of them.

My hands used to bleed when I did this kind of work. Not now. Now my palms were like moving stones, pressing, rolling over the two sections and twining them around one another until they were long enough to tie off a sail.

My younger sister Avi snored lightly on our straw mat in the port tavern's undercroft. I opened her hand. Someday—if I managed to keep her alive until someday—those angry blisters would disappear and she'd have rocks for hands too. I touched the area around the worst of them gently. Though she was four-teen, I rubbed her arm like Mother used to do when we were little. Soon enough, she'd be beside me on the sea, rushing to finish our day's work before the night fell and the salt wraiths came. But she didn't love the risk, the delicious challenge, or the waters like I did.

"Kinneret?" Avi's eyes opened, red and bleary.

"No. I'm Amir Mamluk," I joked, pretending to be the steel-eyed woman who held the town in her ruthless grip, only a few steps below the kyros in power. "I am in disguise as your sister so I can enjoy the pleasures of low-caste life. What's first? Prying barnacles off the hull or watching my hard-earned silver disap-pear into rich men's pockets?" I clapped my hands like an idiot as Avi bent over laughing.

"You're a madwoman, Sister." She looked past me to the light. "You've should've shaken me awake sooner. Did you get your sailing papers stamped?"

I waved her off. "I will. Tomorrow."

"All right." A black spot marred the edge of her grin. She'd lost a tooth last week. The empty place looked wrong next to the pretty yellow-brown hair she'd inherited from Father.

Avi leaned over to touch the shells she hid under her side of the mat. She didn't know I knew about them, so I stood and turned away, giving her a moment. It was her own ritual and whatever gave her peace was fine with me.

Gathering the fibers I hadn't used last night and the new

rope, I forced a worthless tear back inside my eye and tried not to hear her little whispers.

"Mother. Father. The kitten. The cat. My broken bird."

She'd found a shell for each of the ones she'd lost. A curving one with ridges, as dark brown as our mother's skin had been. A spotted one for Father. He would've liked that. He'd loved the unusual.

As I tied on my sash, the tiny bells jingling, she drank from the bucket and wiped her mouth with the back of her hand.

"Eat that bread there." I jerked my chin at the stool that served as our table.

"What about you?"

"I ate with Oron late last night," I lied. I was a great liar, but I didn't rejoice in it. Lying was the skill of the desperate, something I intended to stop being as soon as possible.

"He actually ate?" Avi said around the nub of bread. "I thought he was on an all stolen wine diet."

"He wishes. Said so right before he went down to the boat." This time of year, depending on the crowd at the dock, my first mate sometimes slept onboard to protect our only real possession. Harvest brought a lot of strangers who wouldn't worry about consequences.

Smiling, Avi shook her head and handed me the bag of salt I kept tied to my sash. I shook it, felt its soft bottom. There was enough for some Salt Magic if we ended up needing it today.

"What shipments do we have?" Avi asked.

"None. We're scouting new port locations again."

"Hope it goes better than last time. Is Calev going to predict our weather for the trip?" Avi grinned.

As a member of the native community of Old Farm—and the chairman's son to boot—Calev was born high-caste, raised to oversee his people's lemon orchards and barley fields, and basically treated like a kyros around town. *The brat*, I thought, a grin tugging at me.

But despite his powerful family and his position, he had the hardest time predicting weather, a child's first lesson on a farm or at sea. He just couldn't seem to gather the clues hidden in the thrush's song, the clouds' sudden curl, or the moisture in a breeze. Seriously, he was rubbish at it. His eyebrow twitched when it frustrated him and it was—

"You're the prettiest when you smile like that, Kin."

I shoved her gently. "Shut up, you. Come on. We need to go."

My relationship with Calev was complicated. And dangerous now that we neared the age of adulthood. Avi really did need to shut up about it.

At least until I found some way to snake into a higher caste.

I unlocked the door and held it open for her, pretending there wasn't a pile of both human and animal waste we had to step over. Soon, the middle-caste merchants would open their booths in these dirty streets to trade goods and gossip under the white-hot sun.

Ugh. There was the sailmaker's son.

He was still burned over the deal his father gave me when Calev came along to buy our new sail.

"Kinneret Raza the Magnificent, friend to high-castes." He pretended to whisper, but his words were plenty loud. "But only if you have eyes and a backside like that Old Farm boy, Calev. For him, she pretends that bag of salt at her sash is for seasoning food. It's a miracle he doesn't see you for what you are. Witch."

A ringing filled my ears. If the wrong people heard him, we'd wish our only problem was finding something to eat today. "The real miracle is that pest birds haven't nested in your continuously open mouth, between your rotting teeth."

His gaze lashed out at Avi. "Soon I won't be the only one with an Outcast's mouth, witches."

I raged toward him and he lifted his leg to kick me off, but Avi jumped in the way. The tip of his sandal struck her leg, and she winced.

"You better stop it," Avi shouted. "Or you'll be sorry."

He laughed and went on as I bent to check Avi's leg.

"It's a scratch," she said. "It's nothing."

"That horse's back end is going to be nothing if he ever touches you again. You should keep quiet when he is around."

"Oh, like you do, Sister?" She raised both eyebrows.

I snorted. "Well, I'm Kinneret the Magnificent, remember?" The ridiculousness of the title burned like a brand.

Avi put a hand on my arm and pulled me to standing. "You are magnificent to me."

I hugged her and felt her shoulder bones like driftwood under my arms. My temples throbbed. She was little more than a skeleton. A chill slithered down my back. How long could we live like this?

A woman who'd been Outcasted sat at the bend in the road, begging. Bells hung from her knotted hair, the edges of her dung-crusted tunic and sash, from every fingernail. The metal seemed to weigh her down, making her back slump like someone years older, bones rising beneath her rags. As a high-caste man walked by, his five bells lightly ringing, she tucked her feet under her, hiding the scraps that used to be sandals in a series of rickety movements.

The high-caste whipped around and pointed at the Outcast.

In addition to never being allowed to enter their families' homes—or anyone else's for that matter—they weren't permitted to hold a job, wear more than rags, or cover their feet with shoes. At the man's gesture, the woman closed her eyes and removed her sad excuse for sandals, shoving them into the gutter. The high-caste nodded and continued on, obviously pleased with himself.

I'd heard the town's last amir caught her doing Salt Magic to win a boat race where the prize was a hefty bag of silver. But I wasn't going to let that scare me off what my mother had taught me.

An image of her hands covering mine, salt glistening on our skin, blinked through my mind. I could be sly with the magic she'd given me. I could be clever with the way I used it. No one needed to know.

As we started toward the dock, a couple of high-caste women paraded by, their skirts clean and black and beautiful.

One sneered at Avi's skirt. "Filthy scrappers. Look at the blood on her clothing."

The other one frowned. "They were probably fighting like dogs."

Idiots.

I never bought anything that wasn't red just so no blood would show on me. But the high-castes were wrong. It wasn't fighting that normally brought the blood I hid. It was making rope, hauling sail, lifting, scrubbing, scraping. And I'd never let them see my blood.

As we continued on, Avi raised her chin like a proud woman twice her age. She should've had her woman's bleed already. It was lack of food that scared it off. I knew what came next. Her hair would go. The rest of her teeth, her skin.

I knew Calev would gladly give us a loaf of bread or some lemons. But the questions I asked myself were always the same. What about tomorrow? And the day after that? I couldn't beg off him.

No.

I wouldn't let him bring us food every day like we were crip-
ples. The thought turned my empty stomach and I kicked at the
dirt. Mother and Father had made this life work. I could too.
When the fevers had them, I'd promised I'd take care of Avi.
Maybe I'd get another headland farmer to use us to ship surplus
barley across the strait.

But that didn't put figs in Avi's mouth today.

"What are you doing?" Avi whispered as I walked up behind
a woodcutter's cart.

Manure and fresh timber masked the scent of what was
almost certainly a bag of barley cakes near the left wheel—the
woodcutter's noon meal. I threw a tiny rock toward his horse's
back leg. The horse jerked and the cart lurched to the side, the
woodcutter shouting at his animal as I snatched the bag faster
than a falcon can grab a chicken.

I ate one before Avi could argue, hurrying around the cart
and hiding the bag in the folds of my skirt. And though she
frowned at me the entire walk to the dock, Avi ate her fill
for once.

FISH LIVER OIL WAS BOTH THE WORST AND THE BEST SMELL IN
the morning. Best because it meant I was near my boat. Worst
because, well, it was fish liver oil.

The fisherman selling the stuff crossed his arms. "I won't give
it for free."

"But you dump most of it anyway," I argued. "It's rancid."

"You need it. So I want something for it."

Of course he did. This was Jakobden, after all. A port town
full to bursting with people who cared for silver and fame, and
nothing as low as a generous spirit.

"Do we really need it?" Avi asked.

I whispered in her ear. "The stern stitching is begging for a coat."

I felt the coins in my sash. Four coppers. It was all I'd saved toward a better boat, a better sail, a better anything. Then my gaze dropped onto the bag in Avi's hand. There was one barley cake left. It would leave me without a noon meal, but the lack of oil could sink us under the wild waters of the Pass, the strait we sailed every day.

Avi saw my eyes and handed me the bag. I held a cake out to the man.

"Fresh this morning," I said. "It's more than you deserve."

He frowned, then snatched the cake and pushed it into his sash for later. After he ladled some oil into our small, wooden bucket, we headed down the near deserted dock toward the red and purple boat our parents had left behind.

Sitting side by side on the dock's uneven planks, we took turns dipping our brushes into the foul-smelling oil and painting it over the coconut fiber stitching that held the stern in place.

Seawater slapped the space between the boat and the dock as I called out, "Oron!"

No answer.

"Why do we love him again?" Avi asked, grinning.

"If he didn't handle the sails like the Fire, I wouldn't...no...I'd still love him. The beast."

I didn't affectionately call him 'the beast' because he was both a pale-skinned northerner and an unusually small person—I wasn't a horse's back end like the sailmaker's son—but because of his taste for drink, his sharp tongue, and his tendency to nap like an oversized cat.

Footsteps pounded down the boards, and I turned to see an official striding toward us, his tunic and sash billowing in the wind. Worry tied a neat knot around my heart. This might be about the rent and what I owed. It might be about any number of crimes. And the Fire knew, my word against a middle-caste's would be mouse dung to silver pieces.

Avi dropped her brush into the water and her lips pinched together. "I told you we should've gone for the stamp and seal."

I groaned as the I helped her fish the brush from the water. These dock officials were the worst.

"Just *Kinneret* them," Avi whispered. "Like you did to the woodcutter."

"Hush," I said, shaking my head.

"Sailing papers," the official spat, looking down at me.

Standing, I gritted my teeth and pulled my out-of-date papers from my sash. "Everything is good here." I held them to his face, then quickly folded them again.

He ripped them from me. "These are expired. You cannot sail again until you have an updated stamp. Report immediately to the town hall." Spinning, he hurried back up the dock.

"Guess I'll finish this up while you go," Avi said. I didn't like how she looked. The skin around her mouth was pale.

"I don't want to leave you."

"You have to. You know you do."

"I'll kick Oron awake first," I joked. Sort of.

He may've been the one who came to us in our worst hour, and close as an older brother or an uncle, but he still needed a good shove every once in a while.

She stood and wiped her hands on her skirt. "I'm fine. I'll do it. Go."

I had to smile. She sounded like Mother.

I rushed away, hoping she really was as strong as I thought she was, and praying my own stubborn will might be enough to keep us from the life of a dead-eyed beggar.

Get Waters of Salt and Sin and read the rest of Kinneret's story for romance, adventure on the high seas, and unique magic!
Available on Amazon and in Kindle Unlimited today.
Also, stick around for a Scots slang dictionary!

SCOTS SLANG DICTIONARY

approved by Thane Campbell

aye—yes

    bampot—a fool who is sometimes amusing

    bairn—baby

    beamer—red face from embarrassment usually

    ben—mountain

    bide—wait, live, stay (depends on context)

    blether—(sometimes spelled blather) talking on and on, chatting

    boak—(sometimes spelled boke) vomit

    boggin'—dirty, no good, smelly

    bonnie—beautiful

    bowfin—dirty, smelly

    braw—beautiful or brilliant

    canny—clever, shrewd

clipe/clype—(varied spellings and usages) a tattletale, a rat, to tell on someone

close—a covered alley

coo—cow, usually a Highland cow (they are adorable so google that)

crabbit—grouchy, mean tempered

daft—stupid but usually harmless

dinnae teach yer Granny tae suck eggs—Don't try to teach someone something they most likely already know

doister—big storm, rain big time

dreich—wet and cold weather

feartie—coward

geggie—mouth

glaikit—dumb, foolish

Glasgow kiss—headbutt

gob—mouth

hackit—ugly

haud yer wheesht—hold your wheesht (varied spellings) Be quiet

keek—a quick look at something

ken—know

kip—nap

manky—smelly

mawkit—dirty

muckle—a good amount

numpty—stupid person

pure—very, exceptionally

skelp—slap

skinny malinky longlegs—skinny person

sleekit—clever, sly (negative connotation)

stramash—a scuffle, a chaotic tangle of a bother

tattie—potato

tidy—lovely, good, beautiful
wean—child

**I hope you enjoyed some fun Scots slang!
Now go grab *The Edinburgh Fate* (Spring 2018)and read
the rest of Thane and Aini's story!**

www.ingramcontent.com/pod-product-compliance
Lightning Source LLC
Chambersburg PA
CBHW051244250626
47155CB00009B/3158